MW01172022

LOST IN LINC

CAINE & GRACO SAGA 3

E.M. SHUE

E. M. SHUE

LOST IN
LINC

Caine & Graco Saga Book 3

E.M. Shue

E. M. SHUE

LOST IN LINC

Cover Design by Leah Holt of Always Ink Covers

Editing by Nadine Winningham of The Editing Maven

www.authoremshue.com

emshue.ak@gmail.com

 Created with Vellum

For my Aussie PR girl

Rylee

CHAPTER
1

The overhead bins shake and rattle as the plane lands. I hate flying. I grip the armrests tightly and push my body into the back of the seat. I *really* hate flying. I wouldn't be doing this if I didn't have to. But in order to make it to the interview on time, I couldn't drive or figure out some other travel arrangements.

"Welcome to New York City." The flight attendant's voice comes across the intercom. "The current time is two twenty. Weather is sunny and seventy-two degrees. We'll be pulling up to the jetway shortly. On behalf of all your flight crew, thank you for flying with us today."

After the door opens, I stand up in my four-inch platform high heels. The black with a pale pink bow shoes are one of my many favorites. Back home in L.A. people don't turn to stare at me, but here several people turn to look at me as I step into the terminal. I ignore them.

My long dark brown hair is up in a retro bumper bang with victory rolls on the sides. The back is pulled up into a curly loose bun with a red bandana wrapped through it to finish the look. I'm wearing a pair of jeans rolled up and a black T-shirt that accentuates my double D's. My makeup is on point even though this was an early morning flight. I don't leave my house without it. My bestie calls it my armor, but to me it's just me. Maybe it's the product of being raised by a plastic surgeon in the nation's land of beauty among all the movie stars, but I've been like this since I was a teenager and learned about makeup.

I pull my carry-on behind me with my purse over my arm as I make my way to baggage claim. I don't travel light, even though this was only for a weekend. I wasn't sure what my mood was going to be after the interview. I watch the vintage Louis Vuitton suitcase come around, and my heart races with a bit of nostalgia as I reach for it. The whole set

I'm carrying was my mother's. It was her first splurge buy after she got her medical license. I wanted her and my daddy to be here with me on this trip, and this was one of the ways I could make it happen. I pull the strap out of my carry-on to attach the bags.

With no time to check into the hotel before my interview, I look for the nearest restroom and make my way to it. I need to get ready quickly then grab an Uber or a cab to the clinic. After a quick check, I find the handicap stall empty. It's spacious enough to accommodate my luggage and allow me room to change. I open my suitcase and pull out the towel I had left on top. After laying it down, I slip off my shoes and step onto the towel so my feet aren't directly on the dirty bathroom floor. I grew up in L.A., I know what happens in bathrooms.

I change out of my jeans and T-shirt. Then I slip on the garter belt and hose, and slide the dress over my head. The vintage Vogue houndstooth pattern skirt is high waisted and lands at my knees; the attached black shirt is long-sleeved and zips up the front. I pull out a bag with shoes in it and remove the red plaid ankle wrap platform shoes. They are four inches high, giving my five-foot-four curvy frame some necessary height and making my legs look killer. Well, and my ass too. I smile. They were purchased just for this interview.

I pull out my makeup bag and close my luggage before stepping out of the stall. After a quick check for smudges from my winged eyeliner, I apply a fresh coat of red lipstick and some added blush to my cheeks, then I move on to hair. I pull the scarf off, followed by the ponytail holder holding up my bun. My curly hair falls down my back, and I wet my hands to scrunch the curls back to life. I leave my hair loose and look at myself in the mirror.

Taking a deep breath, I pull my shoulders back and calm my nerves.

I'm overly qualified for this position, but it's a dream for me. No more being strictly a team physical therapist. I would be working for a large practice known for sports injury and recovery. *It's yours to lose*, I hear my parents in my head. They always said every job I interviewed for was meant to be mine, it was just me losing it on my own. I got this.

I walk out of the restroom and head for the exit when I notice a man in a black suit with a sign that says, "R. Parsons." That could be me. He's tall, bald, and fairly muscular.

"Um, excuse me, I'm Rylee Parsons."

"From California?"

"Yes, sir." I don't know why there would be a driver waiting for me.

"Hello, Ms. Parsons, I'm here to get you to Dr. Overmyer's practice." He reaches for my bags and I let him. I keep my large purse and nod at him.

"I didn't know the practice was going to provide me with a driver. Thank you."

"I was sent by Mr. Olson Rodgers. My name is Ray. I was just about to give up on you, but I called Mr. Rodgers and he told me to wait a bit longer."

"Oh, I stopped to change after I got my bag."

My bestie, Ollie, was worried about me coming to New York by myself. He's been taking care of me for months now. When he found his new job here that he starts in a few months, he wanted me to look for a job here too. He doesn't want to leave me alone in L.A. where he thinks I'm still in danger. Besides, I've always wanted to live in New York, just like Carrie Bradshaw. It was my dream, and after I lost my parents, I knew I couldn't stay in L.A. any longer. Too many memories. So here I am, trying to follow my dreams. Along with Ollie.

I smile at the driver as we step outside and head to the parking lot. He walks up to a Mercedes sedan and pushes the unlock button on his key fob. He opens my door and I slide into the back seat. He climbs into the front after storing my luggage in the trunk.

"I'll keep your bags with me until I take you to your hotel. I'll be your driver all weekend while you're here in town." He looks in the rearview mirror at me.

"Thank you. I'm not sure how long this will take."

"Mr. Rodgers gave me your cell number. I'll text you so you'll have mine and then you text me when you're done."

"That would be perfect." I smile at him as I pull out my cell and text Ollie.

Rylee: A driver? Really? Are you afraid I'll get lost?
Ollie: I'm looking out for my bestie. Just be nice to him. No sleeping with him or flirting. He's your bodyguard too.
Rylee: Really? Darn you take away all my fun. Thank you. I love you.
Ollie: Good luck. It's yours to lose.

I slip my phone back in my bag and watch as we drive into Brooklyn then cross over into Manhattan. A bodyguard? There was a time when I didn't think I needed someone like that, but now I'm not sure. Between my parents' deaths and the weird things that have been happening, I understand why Ollie is concerned.

I start to get more nervous the closer we get to the clinic. I rub the bracelet tattoo on my left wrist and think of my parents. How much they had prepared me to do this. How proud they would have been that I'm jumping out of my comfort zone. How much I miss them.

When we pull up to the curb, I take a couple deep breaths and grab my large tote as I wait for the driver to open the door. I step out and take in the multistory facility. This isn't just a physical therapy center, it's a full-service sports injury and recovery center.

This is mine to lose.

❧

AN HOUR later I'm walking out to the curb again and sliding into the back of the car. Mine to lose alright! Ugh!

I pull out my phone and call Ollie this time. I can't say this through text.

"How did it go, Leelee?" His soft voice comes across the line.

"Well, if it was just Dr. Overmyer, I'd have walked out with the job." I huff.

He sighs. "What happened?"

"The office manager, Veronica, was in the interview." I huff again. "She took one look at me and judged me as a floozy right away. Everything is covered, Ollie. The girls are put away. I wore what you helped me pick out. I didn't do my makeup too dark. I even left part of my hair down. What did I do wrong?" I shake my head and whine into the phone.

"Leelee, sometimes women don't know how to react to someone as beautiful as you."

"She saw my bracelet tattoo and asked if I understood how uncomfortable I would make patients with my visible tattoos. I told her that no one is uncomfortable with mine because they are all tasteful, but I offered to wear long sleeves, even in the summer if necessary. I'm not changing who I am for them, Ollie." I sigh. "She was upset I wouldn't tell them which team I work for in Cali. I told her about the NDA, but she didn't care. She asked how she was expected to confirm my employment. I told her to call the number I provided and they would confirm." I pull my full top lip between my teeth and worry it. "If I have to, I'll apply with some of the teams here."

"No. No more teams. After that last incident, I don't want you to be hurt anymore. We haven't been able to determine if he's the reason for all your troubles." His voice is gruff as he raises it.

I think of that last situation. All I did was agree with the physicians that a player shouldn't return to the field for a while. I can't help that the team ended up firing him when they found out he was still playing and training with a B-class team. I don't know why he blamed me for that, or the fact he lost the one endorsement he had.

Ollie continues to gripe on the other end of the phone about how working for the teams isn't what will work for me. He tries too hard to sound tougher than he is, and it makes me smile.

"Be careful, Ollie, your guy is coming out. I might have to tell your fiancé you're a switch up." I laugh and Ollie does too.

"Stop it. Paul likes when I get tough."

"Okay, but still, what am I going to do? I can't stay in L.A. without you, and I don't want to work for teams anymore."

"Apply at the hospitals and other PTs."

"Fine." The word comes out with more power than I want it to. It's not that I think I'm above working for hospitals, it's just I've done my time on rotation. I'm ready to show what I know.

I reach up and unzip the front of my shirt, pulling the

zipper down to where I would have normally worn it. My cleavage pops out and I watch Ray's eyes bulge for a moment. Yeah, I know I have a nice rack.

"Go get yourself laid. How long has it been now?"

"You told me I can't. Besides, you and I both know how long it's been." The pain in my voice is hard to cover. Yes, I used to sleep around; I'm not ashamed of who I am or that I like sex. But the last time I had a one-night stand my world was shattered, so I changed. I'm looking for someone. I want to settle down. Life is too precious to waste on one-night stands and meaningless sex.

"You're going to be at a hotel all weekend, I'm sure you can find someone to scratch your itch."

"I'm not ready for that."

"Just one more time won't hurt you. Besides, in a city of over eight million, you'll never see him again."

"I can't believe you're condoning this. You're the one that told me I should settle down."

"Yeah, well, I was wrong this one time."

"Wait, say that again." I laugh at him. "I can do this, it's like riding a bike." I smile and hang up as we pull up to the hotel.

The Arthouse Hotel is beautiful and elegant. I can't wait to see the room I reserved. Ollie and I researched this hotel together when he came out for a weekend to spend with his then boyfriend. Paul ended up proposing that weekend, prompting Ollie to move to New York. And now I get to stay here and experience the beauty for myself.

"I'm staying here at the hotel too. You have my number if you need anything, and text me anytime you leave your room," Ray says before he gets out.

The doorman opens my door while Ray gets my luggage out of the back. I take his hand and watch his eyes bug out at my cleavage. Most men don't look me in the eye. My smile is sultry, the red lipstick making my lips look so much fuller. I know what it does to men.

"Ma'am, how can I help you?" he stutters.

"I'm a guest." I continue to smile at him, but I don't feel the need to fully flirt. He's not doing it for me. The doorman leads me to the front desk where a tall blond man is standing near on the phone.

"Listen, Tracy, you promised." I hear the deep gravelly voice and it causes goose bumps to erupt across my skin.

I turn to look at him and he looks at me, his eyes sweep up and down my body. When he looks me in the eye, something in my body shifts. It feels like he's touching me everywhere and yet nowhere at the same time. I crave his touch. I feel my body leaning toward him. His dark sky-blue eyes bore into mine. I take in his broad nose and rectangular facial features; his eyebrows are a darker blond and he has a defined brow. His eyelashes are long and curl up perfectly. Eyelashes girls would die for.

My eyes take him in more. He's in black slacks, a white dress shirt with a thin black tie, and a black jacket. Not high fashion but the jacket fits his arms, the slacks mold to his long legs, and the white shirt is tight across his chest. He smells like clean man and a men's product I recognize. The bergamot and sage over cedar and leather. He would work. My nipples tighten and my panties dampen in reaction to him, but then I hear the woman on the other end of his call screeching at him.

Oh well, he would have worked but he's married, and from the sounds she's making, she's pissed. His loss. I flip my hair and turn my attention toward the check-in counter.

"How can I help you, ma'am?" the desk clerk asks.

"I have a reservation."

"Name?"

I give her my name as I smell him again, right behind me this time. His body is close enough that I can feel the heat coming off of him. I swing my head around to tell him to step back.

Linc

CHAPTER 2

The smell of cherries, almond, and a mixture of flowers invades my nostrils, and not in a bad way. I watched her legs as she got out of the car, and I wanted them wrapped around me as I rammed into her against the side of said car. Her wide-set blue eyes are the color of the ocean on a clear, calm day. Her curly dark brown hair swings around and then those bright blue eyes are flashing at me, but I don't look at them. Instead, I take in the heart-shaped face with the full pillowy lips. I can imagine them wrapped around my cock with that red lipstick on them. My eyes wander down to a pair of breasts that a man could fuck, and a waist so tiny you can wrap your hands around. She has hips a man can grab onto as he fucks her from behind. This woman is a sex kitten, and her appearance fits the bombshell pinup beauty.

"Fuck." The expletive rips from my lips as I try not to adjust the raging hard-on I'm now sporting, thanks to her.

"Excuse me?" A perfectly shaped brow rises, and she pulls her bottom lip through her teeth. I want to bite that plump lip. "Please step back." Her voice is husky and sounds like a phone sex operator.

"Babe, you just want me to step back because I'm turning you on just as much." I smile down at her. Her breathing increases and a flush works its way up from her perfect tits to her collarbone.

This little thing is younger than me and could get any man. But hell, I'm going to try anyway 'cause it's the way I am. I get my fair share of pussy at thirty-four, but what I wouldn't give to get this sex kitten in my bed for the night.

"Babe, drinks tonight in the bar. Say eight."

She doesn't say anything but looks me up and down. My already painful cock jumps and my heart pumps harder in my chest.

"What's your name?"

"Lincoln W—"

"No. Just your first name. I'm Rylee."

"Linc. What do you say?"

"Step back and give a girl some room."

"Babe, if I step back, every guy in this lobby is going to think you're for them when you're meant for me tonight."

"Here are your keys, ma'am," the desk clerk says, interrupting our banter.

Fuck, I haven't spoken to a woman like this in a long time. My only focus lately has been work and my daughter. But this weekend is my best friend's wedding to the love of his life, and I'm going to get it on with this beauty. There was a time I wanted what Noah has, and I'd thought I had it until my ex betrayed me. But I never reacted to her like I have with Rylee, the sex kitten. This woman makes me want to forget everything but her.

Rylee turns to walk away, and I see a man standing off to the side. He hands off luggage to a bellhop and speaks to her for a moment. Then she turns away and starts toward the elevators. I check in quickly and take off after her. She better not be with that fucker. I didn't notice a ring, and any right-in-the-head man that would claim her would make sure she wore his ring...and other marks.

Walking up to her, I don't stop myself from wrapping my hand around her tiny waist.

"Rylee, you didn't answer my question. And who was the guy?" My voice is gravelly and sounds rough to me.

When she looks up at me, her tiny pink tongue licks her top lip. "He's my driver, and maybe I'll meet you on one condition."

"Anything."

"Married?"

E.M. SHUE

"No, divorced," I answer her honestly. "You?"

"Nope, single." She pops the P.

"Then I'm all yours and you're mine for the night."

"Maybe." Her grin is wide and teasing.

"No maybes about it, my sex kitten, I want to know what those lips feel like against mine." I crowd her body as the doors open. She pulls away and steps in, and I follow her, pushing her against the wall.

I've never reacted to a woman like this. I've never wanted to mark. I've never wanted to claim every breath. Yes, my partner used to joke I was a ladies' man, but that was before I'd realized I didn't want my daughter to ever find out how disrespectful to women I was before. But this woman is a siren calling me to her with her body and sassy mouth. Is this what Noah felt when he first met Kenzie?

I press into her and I'm about to kiss her when she clears her throat.

"Push sixteen," she says, and I turn to push her floor then mine.

I cage her in again, and this time I lift her chin up. I need to feel those lips against mine now. I lean down and slide my lips across hers; they are full and plump but so soft. I drag my lips against hers again, then two more times. On a groan, I take them deep and slide my tongue across the seam of them. Her hands grip my shirt and she opens for me. My tongue dances with hers, sliding back and forth, in a dance older than time. My cock wants to be buried in her tight little body.

I pull my mouth away from hers. Her lips are swollen from my bruising kisses and I just want to give her more. The elevator dings and I step back and watch her eyes flutter open. The passion in them almost makes me say "fuck it" and just follow her up to her room.

"I'll see you at eight, or I will find you, sexy." My voice is husky from my desire.

"I'll meet you in the piano bar, Linc. I'll be the one without panties." Her voice is sexy and low, causing my cock to jump again. Phone sex with her would be so hot.

I walk backwards, keeping my eyes on her as I step out of the elevator. Her breasts are heaving from breathing so hard from our kiss. I groan as she licks her lips, taking more of my taste into her mouth.

"Fuck, sexy, eight can't come fast enough." The doors slide closed as she waves her fingers at me, cherry red polish on her nails.

RYLEE

Watching him as the doors close, I almost jump out and follow him to his room. That man is sex on a stick, and I can't wait to jump on him for a ride. I'm glad Ray had to go park the car and didn't follow me in to see me and Linc kissing. When the elevator doors open on my floor, I make my way to my suite.

The large room has an attached deck with a view of the city. A knock on my door has me hoping Linc followed me up here. I walk over without looking out the peephole and smile.

"Hello, I have your luggage." The doorman smiles at me.

"Oh, just a moment," I say over my shoulder as I turn my back on him and walk to my purse I left on the table. I pull out a few bills and walk back over to him. He takes my hand in his and I shake it off not wanting to give him the wrong impression. His smile drops when he realizes I'm not into him. I make sure the door is locked up after he walks out.

I bend down to take off my shoes before heading to the bathroom for a shower. After the long flight earlier, I want to be all nice and fresh for Linc later. I just had a visit at the salon before I left L.A., so I know all my bits are smooth.

AFTER MY SHOWER I use my diffuser to bring out all the curls in my long brown hair. The natural spiral and corkscrew curls fall to mid back. I pull the curls on the sides in front of my ears and back comb my hair to give it more volume, then I roll each into victory rolls, leaving the very front out. I use just enough spray to make them stay but not make them crunchy. I then take the very front and manipulate it into a curl that I pin over the front of the victory roll on the right side. It makes a pretty effect. I leave the back down in curls and add a flower over my ear on the left side.

My eyes are winged with a bit of shimmer shadow on the lids. I darken my brows and color my lips red. Making sure my robe is cinched tight, I walk out to the living room and grab the room service tray I'd ordered earlier and place it out in the hall. I return to the bedroom and slide the robe from my body, then slip the black dress up, settling my full breasts into the built-in bra before zipping it up. I cinch the belt, making my small waist look smaller.

The dress has thick straps over a sweetheart neckline and goes to my knees. My full sleeves of tattoos are visible. Wonder Woman and Harley Quinn as bombshell pinups are on one arm with other fun colorful art between them. My other arm has a bombshell tough girl Rosie the Riveter and a pinup Snow White with the words "I'm waiting for true love's first kiss." The tattoo on my wrist is a rosary with "Drs. Parsons" inked in delicate script. The tattoos on my hip and thigh won't show in this dress.

I slip on my black platforms with red cherries and tied with a red bow on the top of my foot. Looking at the clock, I see it's still fifteen minutes to eight, so I grab my black wallet covered in cherries out of my purse and prepare to head out. I like cherries. My car is painted cherry red, and I even have a couple cherry tattoos interspersed between the other tattoos on my arms.

I need to get a drink to calm my nerves before he shows up. I text Ray to let him know I'm heading to the bar, and Ollie to also let him know. It's a habit I started six months ago. After no one could reach me when my parents were killed, I've decided I won't let that happen again. Plus, it means if something happens to me, they will know where I am. Safety was never something I used to think about, but now it's becoming second nature to me. I've taken a couple women's self-defense classes. I learned to shoot too, and I got a conceal and carry permit. As someone who works in the medical field, carrying a weapon and potentially shooting someone is something that took me a while to justify in my mind, but it was something I needed to do to make myself feel safe again.

The whole way down to the main floor I think of how attracted to Linc I am. I've never been this attracted to a man before. It wasn't just his eyes or his body. It was the way he made me feel desired. The way he made me feel safe, something I haven't felt in a long time. The way he gave me his undivided attention. Even though my parents loved me, they had very important jobs and sometimes I felt like their patients got more attention than me. But when they did take time off, I was their sole focus. I push the thoughts of them to the back of my mind not wanting to get myself down.

Rylee

CHAPTER
3

I walk through the lobby and notice several men turning to check me out. A tall dark-haired young guy with light eyes lifts his chin at me but I continue on, not wanting him to think he has a chance. I've got a man coming to see me. A man I desire.

I enter the bar and cross to the opposite side. I keep my back to the grand piano and face the front entrance so I can see when he comes in. He walks in promptly at eight wearing a blue suit with a white shirt. The shirt is open at the collar and the blue of the jacket makes his eyes even bluer. He spots me and walks right over to me.

"Let's get a booth, sexy." He reaches out a hand to me.

As soon as my hand slides into his, I feel like I've touched a live wire. The hair on my arm stands on end and my body tingles.

He leads me over to a red booth and I slide in with him slipping in next to me. The waitress comes over and I order a refill on my martini while he orders a whiskey.

"Before this goes any further, I want to lay out the rules. No last names. No complications. Only this weekend, no expectations of more afterward." I let him know the terms. I can't do complications right now. I don't know what my future is going to hold for me, plus I *need* the reminder that this is only this weekend. I can't find happily ever after. I don't even know if it exists.

"I don't know if I want to agree to that." His eyes darken and I know he's upset with the rules.

"Then I'm going to leave." I start to slide to the other side of the booth.

He reaches out and wraps his hand around my throat, his thumb strokes my chin. His hold isn't aggressive or even threatening. I still and tilt my head back as he strokes lower down my throat.

"You look sexy as fuck begging for my touch. That dress, those heels, and those tattoos make me want you even more than I did earlier. For right now, I'll give you what you want." His grin is predatory as his eyes slide down my body as if he's caressing my skin. When his eyes come back up to my face, he just stares at me and I feel it all through me.

I want this man and I'm willing to let him slide on the rules. Most guys don't like when a woman dictates the terms of a one-night stand, or in this case maybe a weekend. They like to be the one to walk away, not the woman, but I'm not afraid to tell them what I want and need. I'm confident in myself to know what I want, and right now I want him.

We spend the next two hours getting to know each other without giving too much away. I find out he's been divorced for six years. That the woman screeching on the phone earlier was his ex. He doesn't elaborate any more than that and, of course, I can't demand answers even though I desire them. I put the limitations on us. He does tell me he's with the NYPD but doesn't tell me if he's an officer or what he does.

I tell him I was in town for a business meeting. I don't tell him more. I confirm for him again I'm single and there's no one special in my life other than a bestie.

He touches me everywhere he can as we talk. He either has his hand on my thigh stroking it, or on my neck, my arms, my hands. I'm ready for him to really touch me. I'm squirming in my seat and he is finished with his beer that he switched to after his first glass of whiskey. I'm on water now because I don't want to be drunk for him. I've had two martinis. I'm worried he's going to order another drink and I can't sit through that with his teasing touches. I lean into him and drop my hand into his lap and rub up his thigh until I get to his impressive erection.

"I want you and not another drink." I purr as I look up into his eyes. His jaw locks and he signals the waitress.

"Check, please."

I release him to get my credit card and start to hand it to him.

"Don't insult me now, Rylee, put that away. I asked you for drinks and I will pay." I slip the card away and like his need to control. His need to take care of me turns me on. Back home people know who I am and know I come from money. I don't like paying all the time. I want someone to want to take care of me.

He signs the slip for his room and stands. He reaches down, and as our fingers lace, I feel the connection again. The zap across my skin, the awareness of him, the desire to claim him as mine. Hand in hand, we walk out into the main lobby.

"Every man is looking at you, desiring what is mine." His voice is gruff. "Want to tell me why your driver was in the bar watching us."

I turn back to see Ray sitting at the bar. He nods at me, and I nod back.

"He must have wanted something to drink too." It's a lie but it's the best I can give him. He can't know more than that. This is just for the weekend. He can't know about the real terrors that follow me. That message me all the time no matter how many times I change my number. That Ray is necessary.

"Rylee, does he want you? Is there something more between you two?" His jealousy is coming off him in waves and I know how to calm him. I stop and he turns to look at me. I release his hand and step into his body. My hands slip under his jacket and slide up his chest and around his neck.

"Let's show them all who I'm here with." I pull his head

down to me and kiss him like I've wanted to for the last two hours.

He doesn't disappoint, his hands wrap around my waist and gently lift me up to him. I feel consumed by him and need to feel his skin on mine. He dominates my lips, his tongue tangling against mine, claiming my mouth. One of his hands is on my ass squeezing it and I moan into his mouth. What started as just a kiss to show him I'm with him has turned into a full-on make out session in the middle of the hotel lobby.

"Hey, um, Linc, you might want to take this to a room." A deep husky voice breaks through the sexual haze.

Linc lowers me but keeps one arm wrapped around my waist and the other on my ass. I open my eyes and I'm lost in his. His desire rolls through the depths of the blue like a storm rolling through the sky.

He drags his eyes from me. "Noah. Rylee." I turn my head to look at the man that is taller than Linc. He has dark hair and hazel eyes. There's a thick scruff along his jaw. "Kenzie turn in?"

"Yeah, I came down to get her some stuff. I just thought you might want to take this somewhere less crowded." He turns to me. "Nice to meet you, Rylee."

"Hello." I can feel the blush crawling up my skin and I look down at the floor.

"Come on, sexy." Linc laces our fingers together and we make our way to the elevators. He presses the button for the sixteenth floor, and we make our way up to my room. He continues to hold my hand as we step off the elevator. I slide my room key over the sensor on the door and wait for the green light. I turn the handle and step in.

Before I can ask him anything, he presses me into the wall. He pushes my hair aside and starts nipping and sucking on my neck. I moan and push my ass back into him. He lowers the zipper on my dress and slides it down my body.

"Fuck, no bra and no panties. If I had known you were this naked under here, we wouldn't have sat down there as long as we did."

His hands rub from my hips up my waist, wrap around my body and cup my breasts. He pinches my nipples and pulls on them. Again, I rub my ass against him.

"Please, Linc, let me touch you."

"Me first, sexy, because as soon as you touch me, I'm going to want to be planted balls deep in you."

"Please," I beg again as he continues to pull on my nipples. My breasts have always been sensitive, but his rough palms rubbing them has me glad I don't have panties on because they would be soaked.

He kisses my back and slides down lower, kissing all the way down until he gets to the top of my ass. His hands leave my breasts and he pulls my hips back as he sinks to his knees behind me. He massages the globes of my ass, squeezing them. I feel his face press against my ass cheeks, then his teeth as he bites down on each one. I moan and push against him. I need him so badly.

"Spread your legs, sexy." He growls. He kisses my tattoo on the back of my right thigh. It's a red bow with a garter in black and red. "This is sexy as fuck, Rylee." I feel his breath against my sex and obey him. He buries his face in me from behind; his tongue licks into me and then starts thrusting in fucking me. I push back wanting more, needing him at my clit. His tongue licks through my folds again and teases my clit. I cry out from the contact.

"More. I need more, Linc," I beg him.

"You're about to get it all, Rylee." I feel him stand and

hear his belt clank as he undoes it. He continues moving behind me and I look back to see him covering his cock with a condom. I lick my lips.

"Not this time, sexy. I need inside you. Turn around." I do and he lifts me, shoving my back into the wall and entering me in one long thrust. My head slams into the wall as I cry out from the invasion. He's so long and thick, I feel him everywhere.

"Linc," I cry out his name.

"Say my full name."

"Harder, Lincoln." I demand, and he starts moving harder. I'm not afraid to tell a man what I want or need.

He pulls out slowly and slams back into me. My orgasm that was just on the cusp is now barreling to the end, and I release his shoulders I was holding onto to pinch my nipples.

"Fuck yeah, Rylee." He watches me. "Give me your lips, sexy." He orders, and I lean my head up as his comes down.

His tongue fucks my mouth like his cock is doing to my pussy. He continues thrusting into me and I pull away from his lips, arching my back as the orgasm rolls through me. I cry out his name and tighten around his cock.

He slows his thrusts as I come out of the orgasm and leans forward to nibble down my neck. He pulls out of me and lowers my legs to the floor and steps back. I reach for him, feeling bereft, and try to pull him back, but he continues to step away. His eyes are wild, and I walk on shaky legs toward him wanting—no—needing him more.

He strips the rest of the way out of his clothes and kicks the pile to the side. When I step into him, he reaches out and lifts me up in his arms and is in motion toward the bedroom. He drops me down on the bed and flips me over, then slams back into my body and I cry out louder.

"Lincoln!"

"Fuck yes, Rylee, let everyone know you're mine." He grits out the words through his teeth as he works in and out of my body, slamming into me harder.

He's pumping into me so hard that my arms collapse. I reach between my legs and roll my clit around, getting myself to the edge again. His hand smacks my ass and I cry out. His thrusts become more erratic and I feel his cock swelling more as I come. Colors flash before my eyes and my body locks up from the force of the orgasm. I hear him moan my name and he's pulsing inside me. He stays locked inside me for a moment, neither of us moving as we both try to catch our breath.

When he pulls out, he lifts me up and holds me to him as he collapses on the bed with me in his arms. I don't usually cuddle after sex, but I like to cuddle. I just have never found a man I want to cuddle with. But with his arms around me, his heart beating against my back, his fingers lazily brushing against my belly, he makes me want to stay here forever. To think of more than just this moment. More than this weekend.

My heart clenches because I can't think that. I don't have a choice for any relationship right now. I don't have a job here or a future with a man like him. He's only looking for a good fuck too.

I roll in his arms and my heels click together. I sit up and look down at my shoes. I have no energy to take them off yet. I lie down in his embrace again. His eyes are closed, his long lashes brush his cheeks. I trace my fingers across his forehead, down his scruffy cheek, and across his thin but beautiful lips. He nips my fingers and I giggle.

Linc

CHAPTER
4

I nip her fingers as they trace my lips and her husky chuckle makes my cock jump. I want her again. I need her again. I open my eyes and look into the sea of color flowing through her eyes. For a moment I see it all, she wants more. But am I ready to step out again? Am I ready to trust a woman with my heart after what Tracy did to me? Rylee blinks slowly and I watch in fascination as her eyes cloud over and she is now closed off.

"Let me take care of this condom, then do you want to take a shower?"

"Yes." She sighs as she starts to roll away from me, but I can't have her leave me just yet.

I pull her back and take her lips. I keep my eyes open for a moment and watch as she melts, her eyes lighten just before they close. My lips work over hers, drinking from her soul, needing her more than I've ever needed another woman. I close my eyes and hold her tight to me. When I finally let her go, the flush on her cheeks from her recent orgasm is now brighter against her porcelain skin. I watch as she tries to close herself off again, but I like her open to me. I like being able to see everything in her eyes, and I'm going to get her there every chance I can.

I roll away from her and rise from the bed, my cock hard again as I return to the living room to grab another condom. I made sure I had a whole strip of them just for tonight knowing I was going to have her every which way I could. I step into the bathroom and immediately strip off the used condom, tie the top, and discard it before washing my hands. I then lean into the shower and start the water. Rylee steps up behind me, her hands roaming my body. I turn and she's shoeless now, bringing her down about four inches, and I wrap her up in my arms. Her little body molds to mine. I pick up the condom I left on the counter and step into the shower. She grabs a hand towel and steps in with me.

I watch her, wondering why she has the small towel, then she folds it and lays it on the floor before sinking down on it in front of me. My cock is in her face and my breath hitches as she looks up at me with her eyes full of desire.

"I want your cock in my mouth, Linc." She moans in that phone sex voice and my cock jumps.

"Take what you want, sexy," I say, and she doesn't disappoint.

Her small hands wrap around the base of my shaft, guiding me to her mouth. Her still red-stained lips wrap around my cock, and I want the lipstick to smudge on my skin, marking me as hers, but it doesn't. She licks up my cock and takes the drop of precum on her tongue. She closes her mouth and eyes as she savors the taste, and I roll my head back on my shoulders. She's so fucking hot.

Her lips slide down around my cock and I just want to ram into her hot mouth. She sucks me in and I groan, trying not to come from the intense feelings. It's been a while since I've had my cock sucked this good. I look down and watch her hollow her cheeks as she slides off me. Her eyes so trusting look up at me, and I watch as she cups my balls in one hand while her other hand slides down her body to finger her clit.

I slowly start fucking her mouth. She swallows around the head and I groan as I pick up speed. She moans and the extra vibration, along with her fingers squeezing and pulling on my sack, has me locking my knees as I come down her throat. She continues to suck off all the cum, and when she finally leans back, she throws her head back moaning as she comes from her own fingers. I grab her up and slam my mouth down on hers, tasting me on her tongue. I need her taste too. I pull away and grab her hand that was between her legs and suck off her fingers. She squirms in my arms and I'm hard again, needing inside her.

I grab the condom, rip it open, and slide it over my erect cock. Sitting on the shower bench, I grab her ass to straddle me and slam up into her body. Her nails claw into my shoulders as she arches, throwing those tits in my face. I want them in my mouth but I'm afraid to let her go 'cause I don't want her to fall.

She starts riding me like I'm a bronco, hard and deep. I hold her behind the neck and at the waist as I guide her to ride me harder. Her little moans and sounds are almost my undoing. My sexy little woman is hot as fuck. *Mine?* Is she mine? I almost stutter in my movements from the thought. She must notice the pause because she looks at me with worry in her eyes. I tighten my grip and slam her down harder. She screams and I worry I hurt her until she moans then says my name. I look down her body to the hip and thigh tattoo on her left leg. It's made up of roses with lace and swirls. She has some initials in it, but I won't ask yet.

Fuck, every time she cries out my name, I need to hear it again. The need to have my name be the only name on her lips is overwhelming. The desire to keep fucking her until she tells me she won't leave me is so great I tighten my hold knowing I'm marking her.

I lean forward as I pull her to me, then I lean down and bite right over her left breast. She screams my name as she comes. Her little pussy spasms around my cock and I groan as she drags me over the cliff again. I hold her tightly with my arms locked around her body. Her head rests on my chest. I feel her tongue slip out and lick across my tattoo of my daughter's baby footprint.

"This is hot as fuck. How old is your child?" she asks, and I want her to know everything about me.

"Your tattoos are hot, sexy. My daughter, Samantha, is eleven going on twenty-one." I chuckle thinking of her latest challenges to me. She wants her own cell phone and her mother, my ex, wants to give her one, but I don't want her to grow up any more than she already has. And I know the damage a cell phone can do in a youngster's hands.

"Samantha. I love it."

"Yeah, she's a good kid. She's so smart, I often doubt she's my kid. She wants to be a scientist or a professor. She says a professor is more important than a teacher because they get to wear robes like Hogwarts professors. She loves to read and plays the piano."

"She sounds wonderful. You sound like a proud father. How often do you get to see her?"

I don't ever talk about Samantha to my one-night stands, but Rylee has already become more than that. I want her to know it all and I want to know her.

"I only get her every other weekend and two weeks in the summer. Tracy won't let me have any more time because I work too much."

The water is getting cold, so I stand with Rylee in my arms and set her back on the bench. After discarding another condom, I adjust the temperature to warm, then I help her stand and proceed to wash her off. She washes me with the hotel soap, but her scent washes over my senses; I'm never going to be able to smell black cherries without thinking of her.

I step around her body and head out to the room after I'm dried off. She walks out a few moments later after she puts all her hair up in a loose bun on her head. She's dressed in a long nude colored robe that is so sheer you can see her pink areolas through it. She stops in front of me as I sit on the edge of the bed.

"You're not getting rid of me yet." I drag her closer to me using the belt of her robe.

When she's between my legs, I untie it and open it. She lets it slide down her body in a pool of silkiness. I pull her into me with her breasts level with my face and suck one of her nipples into my mouth. Her hands go into my hair and rub along my scalp holding me to her. She's so responsive to my touch regardless of where I'm touching her, but it appears her breasts are extremely sensitive. She moans and arches into me more. With my hands wrapped around her waist, I lift her as I stand and twist, laying us both on the bed and proceed to make love to her slowly this time. She keeps trying to push me into going faster. She's trying to deny us, and I'm not sure how I feel about it.

I fall asleep with her in my arms, her leg thrown over mine, her head on my chest over my heart.

RYLEE

I come awake to my body floating in between pleasure and sleep. I'm on my back and look down my body to see Linc between my legs. His tongue licking over my pussy. I dig my head into the pillow and moan. One of his thick fingers slips inside me and strokes me, rubbing my G-spot as he sucks my clit into his mouth. My toes dig into the bed, the falling feeling coming from the orgasm on the cusp. As he sucks, he drags his tongue up and down over my clit. One of his hands pinches my nipple and I cry out as the orgasm powers through my body. He knows how to play my body after only one night together. I can't do all weekend with him or he'll have all of me, and I'll let him.

I open my eyes again as I come down from the orgasm and he's over the top of me.

"Good morning, sexy. I couldn't leave without having you one more time. I won't be able to have you again until this evening after the reception."

He thrusts his cock into me, and I rock my head around on the pillow. His hand holds my chin in place and his lips capture mine. I taste myself on him and clutch at him, trying to climb into him. Needing a deeper connection, but not wanting it. His thrusts are deeper, and I wrap my legs around him, holding him closer. He throws his head back as he comes deep inside me in the condom.

I cry out his name again. "Lincoln."

He holds me close to him tight in his arms and I try to keep my heart closed off from the feelings he's evoking in me. The light chest hair over his pecs brushes my nipples and I want to rub my body against him. I can't get enough of him.

"Fuck, sexy, I want you again and I just had you. But if I don't get up now, I'll be late, and Noah will never forgive me."

He told me during drinks and after we got back to my room that his friend, the guy from the lobby, is getting married today. Noah used to be his partner before he left to work for a private security company.

He rolls off me and I watch his tight ass as he walks to the bathroom to take care of the condom. His long legs are muscled but like a hockey player more than a bodybuilder like I've seen on Venice Beach. He returns and bends down and puts on his slacks commando. He slips on his shirt and barely buttons it.

I slip from the bed and wrap my robe around me and make my way over to my luggage to pick out what I'm going to wear for the day. I can't watch him go. It will be the last time I see him and my heart hurts from the pain. I can't see him again. I can't give him what he'll want and need. He has a daughter. He's looking for a woman he can spend his life with, and I'm broken.

I have my back to him and am not aware of him until he wraps his arms around me. He pulls me up into his body with my back to his front. His now scruffy chin rubs against my neck.

"Sexy, you're not going to push me out."

"It was just a night, Linc." I try to keep my voice firm but it catches.

"Rylee, please tell me your last name."

"I can't." I choke out as tears fill my eyes.

"Rylee, I will see you later. I will find you."

"Linc, we've already stepped into territory we said we wouldn't."

"No, you said you would give me a weekend. I want the time you promised me." His hand turns my chin so he can take my lips. As soon as they move over mine, I'm lost. I'll give him anything he wants.

"Parsons." The name slips from my lips when he pulls away.

"I'll meet you in the bar again at nine tonight. That should be long enough. If you're not there, I will come here, and if you're not here, I will find you," he growls before he takes my lips again, claiming me as his.

I twist around and hold his body close to mine. Our lips move over each other's, demanding from the other what we both want. My back hits the wall and it surprises me. I didn't even realize he was moving. His phone goes off across the room and he pulls his lips from mine. He sets me down and steps over to it.

"Yep, I'm awake. I'll see you in thirty minutes." He hangs up and beckons me toward him. I walk to him and he leans down hovering over my lips. "I will see you later, sexy." I nod and he softly takes my lips, like a gentle caress.

I watch him walk out the door as I stand there in the middle of the room while the wall around my heart cracks open.

Rylee

CHAPTER
5

After Linc leaves me I take another shower to try to wash the smell of him from my body, but I still feel him everywhere. My body is riddled with marks from him. Love bites, hickeys, and beard burn. I dress in a pair of black tight capri pants, a black-and-white checkered peasant style shirt, and red platform strappy satin sandals with a bow on the heel.

I spend my morning visiting different tourist sites, then stop for lunch at a New York pizzeria before my appointment to look at a few places. As I look at the homes, I'm depressed and worried over whether I got the job or not. I have the money to be without a job for a while, that's not an issue, but I can't not work. It's me. I love my job. I love helping people.

Ray stays in the car for each of the properties I look at. Some are over the top extravagant and not me. I finally find a really good prospect. It's a townhouse with an attached one-bedroom carriage house, but you would have to enter through the main house to access it. I pull my phone from my purse as soon as I get out to the car and dial Ollie.

"Hey, Leelee, I was wondering if I was going to hear from you today."

"Hey, Ollie. I think I found a place and we can still be together." I moved in with Ollie six months ago when I couldn't return to my house. I couldn't be there without them or after what happened to them.

"Yeah, where? Paul hasn't found a place for us yet."

"It's on the Upper East Side. It's a six-story townhouse with an attached two-story carriage house. Both the townhouse and carriage house are joined by an open patio, and you can also access the carriage house through the cellar. It's all modern and clean lines like you love. The carriage house has a skylight and the master suite is perfect for you two.

There are hardwood floors throughout both homes. The kitchen—"

"Slow down, Leelee, I can tell you're excited. Send me the specs and any pictures you took. I'll talk to Paul tonight."

"There is one problem, but maybe we can figure out something. The only way to get to the carriage house is through the main house." I explain, trying to be calm. The thought of living alone scares me.

"I'll talk to Paul. So, did you scratch that itch?"

"Maybe." I smile. "But it's not a big deal."

"Really, Leelee, then why aren't you talking about it?" He knows me so well. I usually brag or give him details, but with Linc I don't want to. I want to keep it all to myself.

"Linc is different, but it doesn't matter, Ollie."

"Why?"

"Because he has a daughter and he said he was only looking for a hookup, but now I don't know. I'm confused."

"Confused how?"

"He doesn't want it to be only one night."

"What does him having a daughter have to do with anything?"

"Ollie, if he ever wanted anything more, I couldn't."

"Why? I thought you wanted kids."

"I do, don't get me wrong, but I..." I can't say the words.

"You had nothing to do with that. It was a tragic accident and an act of violence you had no control over." His voice is gruff in his anger.

"Ollie, if I had been home—"

"Then you'd be dead too. A random home invasion took them. You had nothing to do with it."

"You really believe that?"

"I have to, and so do you. Now tell me about Linc."

"He's a New York cop. He's at the hotel for a friend's

wedding. He's been divorced for a while. His daughter is his world. He's only a few years older than me, and that's all I want to tell you about him." I smile thinking of Linc with his blond hair and beautiful sky-blue eyes. His body that turns me on and his hands that know where to touch me after only one night.

"Wow, Leelee, I've never heard you talk about someone like this. I'm happy for you."

"But what if I don't get a job here?"

"You will. Now stop and go have some more fun with Linc. Call me tomorrow. I'll be at the airport for you on Monday."

"Okay." I hang up and look at the time. "Ray, let's head back to the hotel." It takes us an hour to get back, and by the time I reach my room, I decide to give Linc one more day.

I slip out of my clothes and freshen up before heading down to the hotel restaurant for dinner. I change into a nude barely there thong and matching bra that pushes my girls up more, then I slip my cream-colored skintight dress on. It has a sweetheart neckline with hearts, flowers, and love words tattooed across the material. There's black at the top and on the straps to offset all the other colors, plus a wide black belt that makes my waist look small and my hips fuller.

I fluff my high ponytail to bounce the curls more, then add a pale pink scarf wrapped around the ponytail and give it a pretty bow. I deepen my eye shadow and apply my red lips. The lipstick stains my lips for an all-day wear, but earlier I had put on a different shade for a bit of a break. All of Linc's marks on my body are pretty much covered, except for one on my cleavage. I apply some concealer to it and smile at myself in the mirror.

I know in my head I shouldn't give him another night

but, in my heart, I need him. If tonight is the last night I have with him ever, I want every bit of time I can get with him. I want to pretend that tomorrow he won't be checking out of the hotel and leaving me. That come Monday, I won't fly back to L.A. and my life there. The life that has been in chaos for longer than my parents' deaths. That was just the straw that broke the camel's back, as they say. I've disliked my job for a while now, but a year ago the reality of it was made clear. I'm ready for a change, and the New York job would be the best for me.

I sit down in one of the chairs to slip on my shoes. The black peep-toe platform pumps have a pale pink trim with a matching pink-and-black bow over the toe box. My hand goes to my belly as I take a deep breath to steady my nerves. I try to relax and find that inner peace that has alluded me for a while. I relax my breathing and reach out for that feeling, but it doesn't come, except last night in Linc's arms. I grit my teeth and stand up and walk over to the mirror. I look perfect.

I ride the elevator down to the lobby and walk over to the restaurant. I'm about to open the door when a sign near the handle stops me. It's closed for a private party. I look through the glass and stop dead. My heart seizes. A beautiful statuesque blonde in a fitted lace spaghetti strap dress turns in the large dark-haired man's arms. Noah. Her dress flares out at the back in a mermaid skirt that floats across the floor. Her eyes are only on him and the love shining from them is evident for all to see. They make a striking couple, her all pale hair and tan skin next to his dark hair and tanner skin. He pulls her in close to his body and my heart aches for that right there.

My eyes roam the room and I see the beautiful blond man in the black tuxedo dancing with a little blond girl in a green dress. The girl's hair is in long curls down her back with braids on the sides. She has flowers woven into the braids. She looks up at him smiling as he looks down and laughs. She is standing on his feet as they dance, and the image clenches my heart. I remember doing that with my own father.

I turn around to flee, unable to pursue anything with Linc because I won't take him away from that little girl, and I end up running smack into someone.

"Excuse me," the cultured high-pitched voice says, and I look at a woman with blue eyes and perfectly coiffed blond hair. "Well, don't you have any manners?" She snipes out and I step back.

"I'm so sorry," I apologize.

She looks me up and down and I feel the chill to my bone. I keep my eyes on her. I know women like her. She judges and thinks she's better than everyone.

"I didn't think this hotel rented rooms by the hour." I don't flinch from her hostility, I've gotten it all my life regardless of what I'm wearing.

"I wouldn't know. But be sure to let the front desk know you won't need an hour." I grit my teeth. She steps back and I watch her eyes as she calculates what to say next.

"For a hooker, you got bite. But this place isn't for people like you. Now toddle off before I call security." I look over her shoulder to see Ray step out of the shadows, but I subtly shake my head.

"Your assumptions are wrong, but you just let me know what kind of person you are with that statement. I belong here more than you do, and my black, platinum, and sapphire credit cards are all the proof I need. But if you need security, I can have my guy help you out." My voice has an edge of haughtiness to it. I know exactly how to shut bitches like her up and it all has to do with my wallet compared to hers. I brush past her, making sure my shoulder runs into her. She would be taller than me if I weren't in my five-inch high heels. I hate throwing out that I have exclusive credit cards, but fuck her.

I walk off and decide I'm done with New York. I dial the airline and change my flight as I head toward my room. I'll get room service.

LINC

A movement across the room and on the other side of the glass doors distracts me from Samantha, and I look out to see Tracy talking to Rylee. I can tell from this distance that Rylee's shoulders are tight. When she shoulder checks Tracy, I know I need to get to her.

"Come on, monkey, your mom is here." I stop dancing and lead Samantha over to the bridal couple to say goodbye.

By the time Noah and Kenzie get done hugging Samantha and thanking her for being their flower girl, I can see Tracy shifting from foot to foot in agitation. She's never liked Noah or his family. She thinks they are beneath her. She doesn't know Noah probably has more money than her new husband, but I'll never tell her. I lead Samantha out to her.

"I should have known they would have their wedding at a hotel where hookers frequent." Her tone is biting. "There was a hooker looking in here. You wouldn't believe, she actually insinuated she has three prestigious credit cards. Anyone can search the internet and learn them. She was dressed so trashy."

I look down at my daughter, who has her head dropped. She doesn't like it when her mother talks down about people. Just like I don't like it. My beautiful daughter, if I could reverse our custody so she spent more time with me, I would, but Tracy's new husband is an attorney and he worked me over in court. Wait a moment, what she said finally breaks through.

"Did you just imply that the woman who was talking to you was a hooker?" I grit out through my clenched teeth. I need to stay calm for Samantha.

"Well, yes. Did you see what she was wearing?"

I kneel down in front of my daughter. "Daddy loves you. I'll see you next weekend. Kiss me, monkey." She leans in and kisses me and wraps her arms around me. I know in a few years I'm not going to have this; at eleven, I'm lucky I still get this.

"I love you, Daddy," she says in her sweet voice.

"Daddy? Really, Samantha, you are too old to be calling him that anymore. Call him Father."

I've had enough of my ex. "She will call me whatever she wants for however long she wants. I'll talk to you soon."

I walk away and head back toward Noah and Kenzie. They are getting ready to leave, which means I'll be able to get to Rylee, because after her run-in with Tracy, I have a feeling she's going to run from me.

Linc

CHAPTER
6

An hour later I'm finally in front of her door. It swings open and I know she didn't look in the peephole because she immediately gives me her back. She's in her long almost sheer robe again. What the fuck! She's answering the door in that. I'm about to let her know how I feel about that.

"Okay, Ray, take that suitcase. I'm going to get dressed and we can head out. I want to go to a hotel near the airport so I can fly out as soon as possible. I'll have my other—"

"The fuck you say. You said the weekend and now you're running," I growl as I cage in her body against the wall, her back to my chest.

"Linc," she blurts out.

"Yeah, me, baby. Why?"

"We can't do this anymore. It was fun while it lasted." She tries to deny us.

"Fun? Do you want to see fun?" I'm about to untie her robe when a knock sounds on the door. "Don't move, sexy." I order her as I walk over to the door. I swing it open after I check the peephole. "She's changed her mind. She'll text you later." I don't give him a chance to respond and slam the door in his face.

I grab her phone from the table and text him from it, otherwise he'll keep pounding on the door like he is now.

Rylee: Changed my mind. We're staying here. I'll let you know when I need you next.
Ray: I need to verify this is you. Code word?

Well that was smart of him.

"Rylee, tell him you're staying. What's your code word?"

She looks over her shoulder at me, still with her body pressed to the wall. I love how she obeys me. It makes my dick harder thinking of her submission to me. I watch as her eyes drop and she chews on her lip.

I stalk over to her and press my body against hers, rubbing my erection into her back so she can feel it.

"Give me tonight. Tell him, please," I beg her. I need her. I need her to want me.

"Hockey," she says quietly, and I text him the code word. The knocking stops and I toss her phone on the table again. I watch it slide and go over the edge to the floor.

My arms wrap around her, untying the robe so it can glide down her body. I spin her around to take her in. She's in a tiny thong and a soft cup lace bra that barely supports her. The bra ties between her breasts and is sexy as fuck.

"Why would you answer the door dressed like this?"

"He's just my driver," she says.

"He's a man. You're a beautiful woman."

"Linc, please," she begs me. Her legs rub back and forth, her skin flushes, and I know I can't deny her anymore.

I step back and watch as her breasts heave from her desire. I slip off my jacket and toss it on the chair, my shirt comes off next after I remove the cufflinks. I reach for my wallet and pull out a condom before I release my belt. She's watching me the whole time, her body squirming against the wall. As soon as my pants drop, I kick off my shoes and kick the pants aside, not caring about them.

"Strip and touch yourself." I order, and she doesn't disappoint.

She unties the bra and lets it fall down her back. She then turns, giving me her ass as she slips her fingers into her thong and slides it down her legs. She wiggles her ass and I bite back a groan. When she turns back around and leans against the wall, one hand goes to her tit and the other to her pussy. She pinches her nipple as she rubs her clit. Her back slides against the wall. Her head thrown back as she moans, but her eyes never leave me. I slip my thumbs into the edge of my boxer briefs and drop them to the floor before I fist my cock. Rubbing it from base to tip, my grip tight, the drag of my dry hand gives me just the right amount of friction that I lock my knees.

She's hot as fuck as she continues to tweak and pinch her nipple. She lifts the full weight of one breast and massages it.

"On the bed, on your back, in the middle." I know what I'm going to do to her.

I order her again and she walks past me to the bedroom, lying down exactly as I instructed. I crawl up the bed and over her body. Bracing my knees on each side of her chest, I reach for the headboard. "Suck my cock, sexy."

She leans up and wraps her lips around my cock, sucking me deep into her mouth. The urge to push into her is so strong but I don't want to hurt her, she's so tiny in a lot of ways. I let her take me in her mouth a few more times before I pull back. I look down at her and pray I can control myself through this.

"Hold your tits together, baby."

She smiles slyly knowing what I'm about to do. When she has them pressed together, I slide my cock into her cleavage and rock back and forth, fucking her tits like I've dreamed about doing since I first saw her. I throw my head back at the feeling until I feel moist heat. I look down and her mouth takes in the head of my cock on each thrust. She licks it, and the combined images of what she's doing and what I'm doing to her body have me reciting sports stats in my head to keep me from coming all over her beautiful neck and face.

I lean over and grab the condom I left by her head and

pull away from her to slip it on. When I get to the juncture of her thighs, I slip my legs between hers, opening her up to me. I slide down further and lick through her folds, making sure she is wet for me because I need to be balls deep in her now. What I find is her cherry scented ambrosia waiting for me and I rise up, wrapping her legs around each of my arms as I slam into her.

She cries out from the intrusion and I wait until she looks at me like she's ready to kill because I'm not moving. I smile down at her and fold her over a bit more as I pump in and out of her. Her body responds with more of her leaking from her core. My balls smack against her ass.

"Pinch those nipples and get yourself there because I'm about to give you it all." I demand.

She removes her hands from the back of my thighs where she was holding on and starts pinching her jiggling breasts. I lean down, bending her more, and she holds a breast up as an offering. I take the nipple between my teeth and bite it. Her head rolls back as I watch her eyes do the same, lost in the orgasm that is overcoming her. The flush crawling up her body. She's so fucking sexy when she comes on my cock.

"Lincoln," she moans my name, and I slam into her hard as I come holding myself deep inside her.

I move my arms, releasing her legs but still holding her body trapped under me. Caging her in with my elbows at her head.

When I can finally speak, I look her in the eye.

"You're not leaving me, Rylee. You're mine now." I claim her as I roll to my side and pull her into me, her head resting under my chin and her hand on my heart. I feel the tears on my chest, but I don't acknowledge them. I need to hold her as I think about what I just said. She's mine. I've been fighting it for two days and I'm not going to fight it any longer.

§

I COME AWAKE to an empty bed and the room dark. I jump up and start to panic. Then I see the light on under the bathroom door and hear the shower. I stalk to the bathroom and open the door, then lean against the doorjamb as I watch her through the glass. Her head is bent and her shoulders are shaking. I walk over to her and step in behind her. She raises her face in the water and then turns. I can tell she's been crying.

"Ry, what's going on?" I ask as I tip her chin up to me.

"Nothing," she lies.

I lean forward and kiss her forehead.

"Don't lie to me, Ry. Why are you crying?"

"I'm scared, Linc. I can't do this. I can't take you away from that sweet little girl." Her words rush out, and I pull her into my chest.

"My daughter will still get attention. Until you're comfortable meeting her, we'll spend the weekends together that I don't have her. After that, we'll be together."

"I live in L.A." She looks down and I know she's avoiding looking at me.

"I guess you need to move here because I can't move to L.A. without Samantha."

"I'm already planning on moving here. That's why I'm here. I had a job interview."

"Well, then, we will do the distance thing until you move here. I can do that. Can you?"

"I can't," she says, shaking her head. She won't look me in the eye, so again I lift her chin.

"You don't think you can do the long-distance thing?"

"No, I can't do us. You didn't understand me."

The tears roll from her eyes and I rub them from her cheeks. Her eye makeup is all gone and I'm looking into her clear beautiful face and eyes that always trap me in. I want forever with her and I know I'm ready to try again. After Tracy, I thought I never would be again, but Rylee changed everything. She blew into my life and made me want to try.

"Let's get out before you get too cold." The water is slowly growing colder. I reach around her and turn off the water, then step out and hand her a towel.

Once she's dried off, she slips her sexy robe back on her body. I grab my briefs and put them back on as I lead her to the living room. I don't allow her to sit in a chair by herself but with me on the sofa. I turn and pull her into me. Her head falls back on my arm and she looks up at me. I don't know how I got so lucky to meet this woman, but I'm not letting her go. I still need to talk to her about what Tracy said, but first I need to work through whatever has her upset.

"Linc, my parents were murdered six months ago. The police believe it was a home invasion." Her eyes fill with pain as she finishes and my arms spasm around her.

"I'm so sorry, Ry," I whisper as I lean forward and kiss her lips gently.

"I was supposed to be home with them, but I ended up spending the evening with someone. I know if I had been there they wouldn't be dead."

"Shh, baby, you can't control—"

"I couldn't take it if I took you away from your daughter. I miss my daddy and I don't want Samantha to grow up without you."

I lift her up and carry her to the balcony door. I open it and hope it's not too chilly.

"Wait right here." I sit her on the chair and step back into the suite to drag the comforter off the bed. I carry it out and have her stand, then I sit in the chair with her wrapped in the comforter. She's on my lap with her legs over mine. Her ass on my cock.

"Why are we out here?" she asks.

"Shh, listen." I press a finger to her lips.

The normal sounds of busy New York wash over us. Cars honking, sirens going off in the distance, people yelling and talking on the street. All the sounds I've loved for years, the sounds of my job.

"Do you hear that?" I ask her as I tilt her face to look at me. She needs to know what she's getting into with me. She nods her head. "Most mornings I wake up and dress in slacks and a wife beater, over that I put on a bulletproof vest and then my dress shirt. Some days I don't and I slip on the vest whenever I'm not in the office. Every day I have the potential of being shot on the job. Every case could lead to my death if I'm not careful. Samantha was born after I became a cop, she knows what I do for a living."

"Is that why your wife divorced you, because of the threat of losing you?" she asks, and I know I need to be completely honest with her.

"No. Tracy divorced me because she wanted bigger and better things than what a cop could give her. She wanted a life that a cop couldn't provide. She cheated on me with her new husband." The dawning recognition in her eyes at my truth has her nodding.

"So, you don't trust very well," she quietly says.

"Don't give me a reason to doubt you, Rylee, and we'll be good. So now you can tell me why you won't do long distance, because all your reasons so far are shit." I hold my breath, needing her to answer me honestly.

"Okay, Linc, I'll try." She sighs, and I take her mouth.

She twists and straddles me, and I open her robe under the comforter. My hands rub her breasts, squeezing her nipples. I lean forward and take one in my mouth and suck it deep. She rubs her core against my cock. I groan because I can feel her getting wet for me through my briefs. I pull off her nipple and switch to the other. Taking it between my lips, I gently bite it and she cries out with her head thrown back. She starts to let the comforter slide off her body. I pull back and slide my hands up and pull her mouth back to me.

"Don't let that comforter fall, sexy, because I'll go to jail for killing anyone that sees you like this," I growl, and her eyes fly to mine. She grips the comforter and holds it around us with her arms wrapped around me.

She continues to move over me, and I want to be inside her. I reach between our bodies and slide my briefs down under my cock. I wrap my hands around her waist, lift her up, and impale her on me. The heat is so intense, I can feel everything. Using my grip on her waist, I help her ride me. She rocks over me. Lifting slowly and slamming down. Her breasts jiggle in my face and I lick and suck on them, throwing her over the edge as she orgasms. Her juices slide down my balls and it spurs me on to get her to come again. I lift my hips as I drop her back down on me. My balls pull up, but I need her to come for me one more time. I lean forward and lick her neck, then suck her earlobe into my mouth as I continue to work her on my cock.

"Tell me you're mine, Rylee." I demand.

She shakes her head and I slow down my pumping. She already told me she would try, but I need her to say she will be mine. I need to hear it again.

"Say it, Rylee." I hold her from her orgasm. I can feel her fluttering around my cock ready to come. I lean in and suck a nipple into my mouth again, and bite it.

"I'm yours, Lincoln. Only yours. Lincoln." She cries out, her screams blending with the noises of the night. My name on her lips causes me to come hard inside her. She falls forward on my chest, her breathing ragged, and I hold her to me feeling both my cum and her juices slowly leaking from her. Fuck, I forgot a condom. Well, good thing she said she's mine, because I'm never using a condom with her again. If I got her pregnant, she would have to stay with me. Instead of that thought freaking me out, I'm comfortable with it. I want her to be mine forever. Just the two days I've had with her have proved to me that she is meant to be mine.

I look down and see her eyes are closed, so I carefully lift her up and carry her into the bedroom again. I pick up our cell phones and set them on the night table. I wash her with a cloth and slide in next to her after I retrieve the comforter from the balcony. I take care of her like I've been craving to do for a woman for a long time.

As I hold her in my arms, I think of all the logistics. My apartment isn't that big, but she could come stay with me until she finds a job. I know from just being around her she is used to a wealthier lifestyle, but I know she is nothing like Tracy and doesn't need it. I'm worried about her PTSD from her parents' deaths. I need to talk to Noah to see if he knows of any counselors who could help her. I will also call the LAPD on Monday to get the info on her parents' case. Maybe I can help her get closure.

My arms tighten around her and I'm glad I got to her when I did. If I had waited until our nine o'clock date, she would have been gone and I would have missed her.

She murmurs in her sleep and cries out. I kiss her forehead and she settles in next to me. In the morning, I don't have to rush out. I'll just go grab my small bag and spend the day with her. I can show her my favorite parts of the city. For the first time in a long time, I'm looking forward to what the next day is going to bring me. Maybe I need to see about transferring out of my unit or just going to work for Noah.

I fall asleep content and happy. She and I have a future, I'll make sure of it.

Rylee

CHAPTER
7

The tinkling sound of my cell stirs me from a deep sleep. I feel a heavy weight across my waist and as I try to pull away, he pulls me back into him again. I smile as I turn and grab for my cell phone on the nightstand. With blurry eyes I open my phone and look at the message on the screen.

Unknown Number: Where are you at, Rylee? You can run but you can't hide from me.

My heart stops because I haven't heard from him in a few weeks, not since I changed to this new number. My reality comes crashing back around me. The reason I can't have Linc and Samantha in my life. The reason I should leave Ollie and Paul too. I've been hiding the fact that I've been getting messages from an unknown number since before my parents were killed. This is how I know their deaths are because of me. He told me.

I can't block him because I'd have to block all unknown numbers and I can't do that. I'll have to destroy and get rid of this phone now and come up with another lie for Ollie as to why I need a new cell phone number. Ugh.

I start to pull away from Linc but again his arms tighten. Maybe I can come up with an excuse so he doesn't know I'm going to run. My bags are still by the entrance. I have my robe and the outfit I had planned to wear before Linc interrupted me. All my makeup is packed and only a pair of flowered blue-and-pink platforms sit waiting for me to slip them on. I roll back toward him and kiss his chin.

"I need to use the bathroom, Linc," I whisper, and his arms release me. Phew, that was easier than I thought.

I roll out of bed and head for the bathroom, scooping up my robe on the way. I'll grab my clothes and get dressed quickly when I get out. I use the bathroom and realize we didn't use a condom. I'll need to get the morning after pill since I'm not on any birth control right now. I'm usually not so mindless with need that I forget but Linc does that to me. I want him.

"Hey, sexy, get your curvy, beautiful ass over here," Linc's sleep gruff voice says from the bed when I exit the bathroom. I jump and squeak. "Sorry, Ry, didn't mean to startle you but I missed you. I want to fuck you hard then get some sleep, I'm exhausted. In the morning, I'm going to show you around New York from a true New Yorker."

Shit. Shit. Shit. I need to figure out something. I have to get away from him. He's tired, so maybe I can use that against him. I'll let him have his way with me, then I'll take off once he falls asleep.

I walk to the bed swaying my hips as I watch the sheet tent from his cock. He pulls me to him when I get close enough and kisses me. I lose myself in his kisses and his touch again. When he rolls me under him, I open to him, but he pulls away.

"Roll over and get up on your elbows and knees. Show me that fucking fantastic ass of yours."

I do as he says. His commands control me in ways that I've never felt before. I want to be dominated by him. I want to let him take the lead; I don't need to because he already knows what to do to my body.

He kneels behind me and slides into me. He makes me feel so full and I feel every part of him. I drop my head to the bed and moan in desire as he pulls out and slams back into me. I was primed and ready for him before he entered me from just his kisses.

"Lincoln," I moan.

"Hold on, baby."

He lifts me up by my hips so all my weight rests on my elbows. He pulls my body in hard and I cry out from the deep penetration. Linc continues to pull me on and off his dick, controlling me. His cock is stroking across that spot in me that only he's been able to get without fail every time. I scream as I convulse and climax around his cock, and he fucks me through my orgasm.

He pulls out and rolls me over. "Ride me again." He picks me up and while on his knees, he impales me on his cock.

I do as he says. With my knees on each side of his and my hands on his shoulders, I ride him. But I'm not doing it hard enough for him and he grips my waist, slamming me down harder on him. We both throw our heads back as I feel him deep inside me, his cock pulsing, and again we didn't use a condom.

"Fucking best little pussy I've ever had. You're mine now, Rylee." He wraps his body around me and collapses back onto the bed with me around him. I lie there memorizing everything about him. I slow down my breathing so he thinks I'm asleep. When he starts to snore, I slide off him, and his arms fall to his sides. I brush a bit of his hair back and kiss his forehead. I slip into the bathroom with my clothes this time.

Dressed in jeans, a T-shirt that says "Barbie" on it, and my hair up in a messy bun, I walk back over to the bed. I lean down and kiss him again, praying he stays asleep. I'll never forget him. He's ruined me for every other man.

"I'll always remember you. I could have fallen in love with you." I kiss him again and slip out barefoot, dragging my luggage behind me.

I make my way down to the main lobby where I sit down and slide on my shoes. Trying to hold the tears at bay, I walk past people still milling around the lobby at this late hour and get into a cab. As soon as I get to the airport, I book the first flight I can get on, not caring about the price. I make it into a bathroom to put myself together. For the first time, I don't wear my armor. Why bother when the tears are going to come as soon as I get on the plane.

"WOULD YOU LIKE A WARM WASHCLOTH?" The flight attendant's voice breaks through my silent tears. I peek out from under the blanket and nod at her. "Oh, sweetie, it can't be that bad," she says, and I take her in. She's probably in her late forties. Her long blond hair is pulled up in a tight bun at the back of her head.

"It is that bad." I can't tell her my heart is broken and shattered. I never thought I would fall in love that quickly, but I know I'm in love the further I get away from him. I'll never have what I could have had with him. No man will ever measure up to him.

Linc
3
Months
Later

CHAPTER
8

The file in my desk drawer draws my eye just like it does every time I open it. The first week after I woke up alone in the hotel room, I was angry and drank myself to sleep every night. The second week, I went to the bar and tried to pick up another woman to get Rylee out of my system, but I couldn't even look at another woman. My cock only wanted one woman, and that was my pinup sex kitten. By the third week, I'd had enough and decided to run her name. I called in a favor and got the file that now stares up at me. Her parents' deaths are the only reason I can think of as to why she would want to push me away. I can't find a phone number for her and all her mail goes to a third party. She's hiding. But is it from me or someone else?

I remember she said she'd had a job interview and was supposed to be moving here, but I don't even know where to start looking for her. I've decided to take vacation time after the new year and go out to California and look for her. I'm tired of waiting for fate to put her back in my path. She was meant to be mine and she will be.

"Ready to go, partner?" Rocco's voice breaks me from my thoughts. I slam the drawer closed.

"Yeah, let's get out of here."

After Noah went off on his own, I got assigned this cocky man-child. Rocco's a nice guy and sometimes a good cop, but he's impulsive and unpredictable. He doesn't care for the rules. I've had to hold him back several times from running in with guns blazing. Noah went through a stage like this after his friend Kathryn died, but Rocco is worse. He doesn't like being in the Cold Case division, or the "Old Folks" division, as he calls it. He wants to be in Homicide, but they didn't have openings at the time.

There are days I want to punch him in the face and others where I'm glad he has my back. He's a good detective.

He is also a definite player. Rocco will come in some mornings and change into his spare shirt and use extra cologne to cover the scent of sex and girls from the night before. Looking at him reminds me of where I used to be and glad I've got my life figured out. Now to just get Rylee where she belongs.

An hour later we roll up in front of an address in Spanish Harlem. I look at the area and pause for a moment. "We should call in for backup. This guy isn't going to want to come in after all these years." Forensics finally came back on an old murder case we're working. This guy has been walking free for fifteen years. Plus, it would be safer for everyone. I don't want to worry about Rocco getting out of control and the neighborhood having issues with us.

"Dude, we don't need backup. Come on, this is just an old man that thinks he can get away with murder. We're going to prove him wrong."

I grab the handheld radio and clip it to my side. My sixth sense is telling me this is a bad idea but I follow along as Rocco is already heading into the building. I don't want to leave him to his own devices. Fuck, I hate babysitting other people's kids.

I'm walking up to the door when he pounds on it. "NYPD. Open the door, Mr. Johns," Rocco yells. A gunshot blasts through the door narrowly missing Rocco. He twists to the other side and plasters himself against the wall as the suspect yells out he won't be taken in alive. "Don't make this rough on you, man. We aren't leaving, and we aren't afraid to kill you," Rocco yells again.

"Fuck, man, don't tell him that," I bark at Rocco. I pull the radio and call in our situation and request backup. Then I try to inject some calmness into the chaos next. "Hey, look, Mr. Johns, we don't want anyone to die today. How about you put the gun down and we talk? My name is Linc." I've taken plenty of confrontational situation classes and I know Rocco's technique isn't going to do anything but piss off the suspect more.

"No. I'm not going to prison," Mr. Johns yells back.

"Sir, we think we know what happened, but we need for you to tell us your side. Can I call you Roger?" Again, my voice is calm, but my gun is ready. Sure enough, more bullets tear apart the door.

I wait for the pause in gunfire and am about to talk to him again when Rocco breaks cover and kicks the door in. I grab for him as he fires into the room. The idiot is standing in the open doorway where he's a larger target. We both land inside the apartment and a burning sensation rips through my upper shoulder. I roll and pull the trigger when Mr. Johns pops up from behind an up-turned coffee table, sending the bullet aimed for his clavicle area, hoping I don't kill him. Rocco grumbles and shoots, taking the headshot Mr. Johns was presenting.

"What the fuck, man? You're supposed to have my back, not the perp's, asshole," Rocco yells as he gets up. I stare at the wall now painted with gray matter. I hate taking a life when we don't have to.

"You didn't fucking have to kill him," I growl as I stand up, but all of a sudden everything seems fuzzy. I fall back and groan, then look down at my left shoulder where blood is seeping out. The bullet came through right alongside my vest. I groan again as the pain radiates through me. "Look, fucker." I point at myself. Rocco turns his face and pales as he realizes I'm hit.

"Shit." He grabs for the radio but finds it was damaged when we hit the ground. Using his cell phone, he calls dispatch and gets me an ambulance.

I sit there on the floor and look around at what my world has come to. I can't do this anymore. I want a life with Rylee, and I don't want her to worry about me every time I leave, especially with a partner like Rocco. But I've only ever wanted to be a police officer. I also have Samantha to think about. I don't want her to mourn me, and God forbid, I let Tracy raise her without me. The last few months have been crazy with Tracy pushing poor Samantha to be more mature than what she is. I've been saving money to hire a new attorney so I can fight for more custody. I know Tracy's husband doesn't want kids and hates having Samantha around.

I look over as the paramedics arrive and come through the door. I grit my teeth as they help me onto the gurney.

"We need to roll," the paramedic says to the other officers that are now on scene. They carry me down the flight of stairs and out into the waiting ambulance. I sit there lost in my thoughts and hoping that this is minor, but I know in my gut I'm really lucky.

When the ambulance stops at the nearest hospital, I groan as they maneuver the gurney into the bustling ER. I'm wheeled into a trauma room. The head of the bed is raised as a doctor enters and looks over the bullet wound. My jacket, shirt, and vest were cut off in the ambulance. Fucking out for the money on that suit jacket.

"Okay, Mr. Warren, we're going to prep you for surgery."

"Is everything okay?" I grit my teeth, fighting the pain.

"We need to make sure the artery wasn't nicked. The slug looks like it is in your shoulder blade. We need to repair the muscles, capsule, and retrieve the bullet. Also check to see what bone damage has been done, if any."

"Okay."

He walks out and I zone out as nurses work around me. I

look out into the ER and see a woman I could never forget. She's got a coat in her hand and stands in profile. A nurse is trying to push her back to a room and the words she's saying float through the pain and noise to me.

"Ms. Parson's, for your baby's sake, you need to have an IV and rest. You can't leave."

"Ry." I groan as a nurse pushes me to lie back down. Rylee's head swings in my direction. Her eyes flare wide and I watch as she gasps and starts to collapse when she takes in all the blood. I start pushing people away to get to her, but Rocco grabs her as he enters the room.

"Get your hands off my woman and put her right fucking here." I demand as I point next to me.

RYLEE

"Wake up, sexy." A callused hand brushes the hair away from my face. All my hair is up in a bun at the back of my head today because I didn't want to wet it down. I stretch and hear a groan, causing my body to go on alert. "Careful, baby, I'm a little banged up." Linc's voice is gruff with pain. The memories of seeing him covered in blood flash before my eyes.

I shoot up into a sitting position and my head starts to swim. I fall back against the bed trying to avoid him. After a moment I open my eyes again and blink up at him.

"Lincoln?" My voice is hoarse, so I swallow to gather some spit in my mouth. I'm again pressed up against his body, his right arm wrapped around me.

"Yeah, Ry, it's me. What are you doing here?" His hand brushes my waist.

"I was trying to find you when I collapsed in the cab and was brought here." I confess knowing I have to be as honest with him as I can.

When I got back to L.A., I jumped into life and completely forgot about getting the morning after pill. So, a few months later when I found out I was pregnant wasn't much of a shock. My life had instantly changed at that point. Thankfully, I'd already heard back from Dr. Overmyer's practice and was offered the job. I start the first of January.

"Rylee," a voice yells through the ER and I look toward the door as Ollie barrels in pushing people away. "Rylee, what the hell happened?" He looks at me and then to Linc.

"Who are you?" Linc demands, his voice gruff as he tightens his hold on me.

"Linc, this is my best friend," I say, and he looks down to me.

"Linc? As in *the* Linc?" Ollie asks and I nod. "Okay, I'll step out here."

"Wait! How did you know I was here?" I didn't call him on purpose. He's been a mother hen since I told him I was pregnant and is annoying me.

I arrived in New York two weeks ago after Ollie and I drove from California. I ended up buying the townhouse with the attached carriage house.

"The hospital called me after they got your records from Dr. Tanner. You listed me as your emergency contact."

"Oh, okay."

Ollie turns his full attention to Linc.

"I don't know what is going on here." Ollie waves his hand between Linc and me. "But you need to get her under some control. My heart can't take calls like that." He turns and walks out.

"Your best friend?" Linc's voice is gruff.

"Mr. Warren, we need to get you to surgery," a doctor says from the doorway.

"Just a moment." I start to get up, but Linc pulls me in tighter to his body. "Baby, you better be here when I wake up. We need to discuss this." He nods toward my belly. I'm so excited for this little bundle. The baby is measuring bigger than it should, and with my small frame, I'm already showing at fifteen weeks.

When Linc looks back up at me, I see the questions swirling in his eyes. So I give him the answer he needs and nod my head at him.

"Fuck yeah!" His smile is huge. "Noah, make sure you direct any medical questions toward my fiancée. And make sure she gets an IV to take care of my kid." I look at him like a guppy, my mouth opening and closing. He just called me his fiancée without even asking.

"You got it, brother," a deep voice says from behind me, and I turn to see the large man from the wedding standing next to me. "Let me help you down." He takes my hand and helps me off the bed. I wobble slightly in my heels.

"Be here, Rylee, or I'll tear apart this city to find you. Now give me your lips."

I don't say anything as I lean toward him and allow him to kiss me. But it's over before we both want it to be.

"Linc." I don't know what to say.

"Sexy, you're carrying my kid, so that means you're mine." He shrugs like it's common knowledge and grimaces from the obvious pain from the wound in his shoulder. I shake my head at him and watch as he's wheeled away.

"Come on, let's get you settled and start an IV," a nurse says as she positions a wheelchair in front of me.

"Oh, I can walk by myself."

"You've already fainted twice. I've been informed Dr. Tanner is on his way in to check up on you and the baby."

"I don't need any special attention."

"Ma'am, it's my job." Her hip juts out to the side as one of her hands goes to it.

"Rylee, Linc would be upset if he heard you fainted again. My own wife is pregnant, so I get where he's coming from. Please just take a seat."

"Oh my God, you're just as bossy as he is." I huff as I sit down in the wheelchair. The nurse hands me my bag and my jacket before wheeling me out. Ollie follows us up to the maternity ward and paces the room while I change into a gown and am hooked up to an IV and monitor.

"Um, Noah, right?" I want to make sure I remember his name correctly.

"Yeah."

"You don't have to stay with me."

"Yes, I do. Linc would flip out if I left you. After he almost ripped his partner's arms from his body for touching you, I know you're special to him."

"Don't you dare find this funny." I point my finger at Ollie when he snickers.

"Leelee, I told you men like Lincoln are protective. I knew he would be like this when he found out about the baby."

"Well, I don't want him to just want me because of the baby. I want..." I stop, unsure I want to have this conversation in front of Linc's best friend and a nurse.

"Rylee, he was planning to go to L.A. to look for you. He didn't know about the baby until just a bit ago, so I think that should tell you he wants more than the baby. I work for Securities International, the company Mr. Rodgers here hired to watch you when you were last in New York. I guarantee you if Linc had known you were a client, he'd have been bugging me to get your information. And while we're on the subject, I believe your friend here called today to set up security again for you. You don't mind if I call you Rylee, do you?" He looks between Ollie and me.

I look at my best friend in shock. "Ollie, you promised me you wouldn't make decisions without me again. I told you I would be fine."

"Leelee, I won't get that phone call again, and I promised your father I would take care of you."

"What? When?"

"Before he died. He knew there was something going on. He asked me to take care of you and I told him I would. You're like a sister to me. I won't lose you like we lost them."

Ollie's parents died in a car accident when we were in high school. He moved in with my family afterward. Losing my parents was hard on him too. He walks over to the bed and takes my hand when the nurse walks out. She returns a moment later followed by Dr. Tanner, and the guys excuse themselves so the doctor can examine me.

"Hello, Ms. Parsons. I seem to recall you assuring me I didn't need to rush you into an appointment, that your doctor in Los Angeles was just being overprotective. But you've fainted twice today." His voice is strong and cultured. He's gotta be pushing close to sixty but he's still handsome, even with all the gray in his hair, beard, and mustache. His dark framed glasses make him look distinguished.

I drop my head and try to hide because he's right, I did tell him that. My previous doctor didn't want me moving; every part of my pregnancy has been difficult. But I had assured her I'd found a doctor here in Manhattan and had already set up an appointment.

"Dr. Tanner, I know what I did wrong and it won't

happen again." I had gone out searching for Linc today. But because I never got his last name, each precinct I stopped at couldn't help me. I was too nervous to eat breakfast before I left, and I skipped lunch.

"You can stop right there. I've heard every excuse before, so let's not play this game. Your mother was the same way. She thought her smile would get her out of trouble."

"My mother?" I'm taken aback by his comment. "You knew my mother?"

"I didn't always work in New York. I knew your mother quite well. Your father too, but her I knew better. I also know your new boss. Now, let's take a look at you."

He approaches the bed and proceeds to check over my chart. He looks at the monitors and double-checks the numbers. He then palpates my stomach, causing the monitors to beep.

"I'd like you on bed rest until you see me next Friday. This baby is much bigger than what I was seeing in the charts. You're measuring at twenty weeks. Are you sure about your dates?"

"Yes, sir, I am. I only had sex with one guy in almost a year."

"Okay." He turns to the nurse and gives her some orders before turning back to me. "I'd like to keep you overnight. Tomorrow morning, I want you to undergo a glucose challenge test. For not eating all day, your blood sugar is much lower than it should be. According to your medical history, type one diabetes runs in your father's family. Your blood pressure is also elevated today, and I saw you mentioned it was noted at a couple of your previous appointments."

"Yeah, but I've never had issues and my parents were healthy."

"Rylee?" Ollie says from the doorway.

"You're not the father," Dr. Tanner says confidently, and then looks over at Noah. "Maybe you, but I don't think so either."

"Guys, this is Dr. Tanner, my OB-GYN. Dr. Tanner, this is Olson Rodgers, my best friend, and Noah Caine, Linc's friend."

He shakes their hands, then he tells me he'll check in on me tomorrow before excusing himself from the room.

"I can have Paul run you over a change of clothes if you're staying the night here," Ollie says.

"Yes, please. I have to stay the night. The doctor wants to monitor my blood sugar and blood pressure."

"Why the hell was I directed to the maternity floor? He was my husband and I demand to see him," a voice screeches from the doorway. A nurse backs in holding her hands up, and in walks the woman from the hotel that had insulted me a few months back. "Who the hell are you?" she yells when she spots me.

"Tracy, you need to leave. You shouldn't have been called."

"Well, I was called. By him." She turns around and another man walks into the room. He stands close to Tracy and she touches his arm. They seem familiar with each other.

"Rocco, you shouldn't have called her. Why would you?" Noah demands.

"I want to know what's going on. Where's Linc?" Tracy turns to the nurse, but she doesn't offer any information.

Tracy advances on me and Noah steps in front of her.

"Get out of my way."

"Tracy, maybe we should leave." Rocco shifts from foot to foot as his eyes bounce around the room. I can tell he's nervous.

"No, I'm not leaving. I was his wife and I have no idea who this bimbo is." She pushes her way closer, trying to get a better look at the equipment attached to me. She must not recognize me from the hotel.

Ollie has positioned himself on my other side, blocking the baby monitors from her. I know the second she recognizes what they are because her eyes flare wide and she turns to me with her nostrils flaring. She pushes Noah up against the bed and Rocco tries to pull her back.

"You better not be trying to claim that is his child. I'm the only one with that distinction and you won't be able to get any of his pension. I took as much of it as I could, and I'll get more." She hisses at me.

I've had enough. She's pissed off this momma bear and I'll claw out her eyes before I kick her ass.

"You listen here, you uptight bitch. My baby and I don't need any of Lincoln's money or his pension, we just want his love. I won't ever hurt him the way you obviously have. I care about him and only want him to be a part of our child's life." I rise up on my knees so I can get some height on her. I don't hear the monitors going crazy at first, but Noah and Ollie do because Noah starts carefully pushing Tracy back from me.

"You will never have his heart or his time. I'll take his daughter away from him if he tries to claim your baby."

The threat works and I fall back scared Linc will have to choose between our baby and Samantha.

"As Ms. Parson's attorney, I'm suggesting she stop speaking right now. If you want to talk to her, you will contact my office. As for Mr. Warren, the same goes for him. Be prepared to be challenged for custody of his daughter," Ollie barks out as he comes around the bed pulling a business card from his inner pocket. "Now leave before I have security remove you. You are upsetting my client. And I will press charges against you for child endangerment if it harms her baby."

"What the fuck?" a groggy voice says from the hall, and I sit up to see a nurse and orderly pushing Linc's bed toward the room. "What the fuck are you doing here, Tracy?" Linc asks her as he tries to sit up.

"Mr. Warren, I've advised your ex-wife that you will be seeing her in court. You don't need to speak to her." Ollie steps between Tracy and Linc. "Please go ahead and put Mr. Warren in with his fiancée." He directs the nurse. I don't want to know how many strings he had to pull to allow Linc to room with me. Linc should be on the ortho floor.

I flop back down, upset this has happened when Linc needs to rest and recover. Noah has stayed by my side and now I'm going to need his help. I reach out and touch his arm. He turns to look at me.

"I want him moved to another room," I say quietly so no one but Noah hears me.

"Rylee, he'll be upset." Noah takes my hand.

"I can't be the reason he loses Samantha, she's everything to him." Tears start rolling down my face. Damn pregnancy hormones.

"Okay, let's get him settled and then we'll see." He pats my hand like I'm just being ridiculous.

I huff and turn to look at the monitors. My heart rate is still elevated. I watch the numbers climb when the blood pressure cuff automatically starts up. I try to relax, but I won't allow Linc to jeopardize his custody of Samantha. I turn away from everyone and face the window as they settle Linc into a bed next to me.

"Hey, sexy." Linc's voice is strained and I look over my shoulder at him. His eyes are barely open. If I give it some time, I can wait him out, and when he falls asleep, I'll have him moved to another room.

"Hey." I try to interject some happiness into my voice, but it sounds so flat.

"It looks worse than what it is." Good, he thinks I'm worried about his injury.

The surgeon walks in and comes over to my bed where Noah is standing.

"Mr. Caine, Ms. Parsons, I was able to get the bullet. It entered through the front of his shoulder, skated along the ball of his shoulder tearing up the labrum and his rotator cuff before it embedded in his shoulder blade. He is going to have some nerve damage. Muscles had to be repaired, along with the labrum and rotator cuff. I also repaired the capsule around his shoulder as best as I could. We'll get him started on therapy for the shoulder next week, but I want him starting hand therapy tomorrow morning. I expect him to be here a couple days while we wean him of the IV meds and onto pills. He has a pump of morphine hooked up right now and had a nerve block put in prior to surgery. He's going to be in quite a bit of pain for the next couple of days."

"I'd like Dr. Overmyer to consult on his case." Even if I can't be a part of his life, I want him to have the best care.

"I've already been in contact with his practice. They've suggested twelve weeks time off before he's evaluated to return to desk duty."

"Sounds reasonable." I agree.

"You said he's going to have nerve damage. How significant will it be?" Noah asks.

"We won't know until they start working with him. But due to the fact several nerves were injured, I wouldn't doubt it happening. He should be able to return to full duty, but we won't know until after he completes therapy."

"Okay," both Noah and I say. I look over and see that Linc is asleep now.

"He'll sleep off and on most of the night."

"Thank you, doctor." I lift my hand to shake his before he walks out after shaking Noah's hand.

Now to get him moved.

Linc

Chapter
9

Off and on through the night I woke up and didn't see Rylee. I had figured she was probably told to go home and get some rest. I want her to take care of herself and our baby. But now it's morning and I still haven't seen her.

"Where the fuck is Rylee?" I bark at Noah as soon as he walks into the room. I'm hurting and feel like shit and give him both barrels of my temper.

"Good morning to you too." He laughs in response.

"I'm serious, Noah. Find out where she's living and bring her here. We need to discuss shit."

"Dude, you need to relax and recover. As soon as you're feeling better, you can go after her yourself."

"No, I told her if she left and wasn't here when I woke up, I'd tear apart this city. I'm fucking serious. Go fucking get her or I'm getting out of here."

"Sit back and relax. I know exactly where she is at this very moment, and Kenzie is sitting with her."

"Where?" I bark again.

"How much do you remember of yesterday?" Noah asks me cryptically.

"I'm not in the mood for games. I remember getting shot and I remember finding out I'm going to be a father."

"Do you remember anything from after the surgery?" My brain flashes on Rylee looking so sad. She wouldn't look at me.

"What's wrong with the baby?"

"Why do you ask that?"

"I kinda remember seeing monitors hooked up to Rylee and she looked so sad."

"She is having some complications and the doctor is running tests, but the baby is good, as far as I heard this morning. I figured she'd talk to Kenzie more than me, and they both are talking about babies, so it was a good plan. I have security sitting outside her door; she can't leave without me knowing."

"Why does she have security? And what do you mean outside her door? Of her home?"

"No, man. She's downstairs on the maternity floor. You woke up for a bit when they wheeled you out of there last night."

"Why would they move me? Why couldn't I stay with her?"

Noah's phone goes off before he can answer me. "Caine. Yeah, if she's being discharged later take her home and stay with her until I come by." He hangs up and looks at me, but his eyes are focused elsewhere. He rubs his mustache and beard, a sign that he's contemplating things.

"Well, you going to answer my questions?"

"I'll tell you what I can, and that's all. You're family, but she's a client." Fuck, why did she hire Noah? "Do you remember Tracy stopping by last night?"

"No. Why was she here?"

"Rocco called her. Linc, man, I would be careful, I think they are involved."

"She's not my worry."

"She is when she threatens to take custody of your daughter away from you."

"What?" I'm confused. She already has the maximum she can get without allowing me to see my own daughter, and for that she would need to claim I'm unfit.

"She threatened to take Samantha away if you claimed parentage of Rylee's baby. Right after the surgeon left last night, Rylee had you moved. But congratulations, you have a new attorney."

"A new attorney? And why the fuck would Tracy care if I

claimed my child with Rylee? I would still pay child support."

"I don't know but I'm going to look into it. Ollie, or Olson, whatever you want to call him, is Rylee's best friend. He's an attorney and told Tracy he was representing you."

"That I am," a cheerful voice says from the doorway. "Nice to see you awake. Thought I would stop in and introduce myself, and start the process of getting your files sent to Paul. He'll actually be the one representing you since I have to represent Rylee. I don't want there to be a conflict of interest."

"Represent Rylee? Why does she need representation in my custody battle?"

"First, let me introduce you to my fiancé, Paul Tyndale." Ollie steps aside and a slender man around my height enters the room. He has light brown hair, bright green eyes, and a face women would swoon over. He's dressed in a tailored blue pinstripe double-breasted suit with a flowered tie.

"Hello, Lincoln, I'm glad I can help you. I've heard from Noah that you've been having custody issues with your ex-wife. And now she's threatening to keep your daughter from you. I've already contacted your old attorney and informed him I'm taking over your case. I'll file the motion of appearance today. As for representing you in your case with Rylee, I'll work closely with her counsel." He turns and winks at Ollie. "Even though we both work for the same practice, as long as you understand our relationship, it's not considered a conflict. He and I won't discuss anything other than what pertains to the case."

"Wait. Stop." I shake my head and hold up my right arm to get him to stop talking. "What case with me and Rylee?"

I look at Ollie standing at the end of my bed in a

tailored brown suit and striped tie. He is the same height as Paul. He too has brown hair, a shade darker than his fiancé's, and his eyes appear hazel. He gives me a smile but I can tell it's forced. He lifts a soft briefcase and pulls out a stack of papers and hands them to me. I look down at the title. "Notice of Termination of Parental Rights" is in bold print.

"What the fuck is this?" I yell and neither man steps back.

"Rylee wanted to make sure you knew you could see the baby whenever you wanted, but she thought this would be the best outcome to ensure your case against your ex-wife, Mrs. Adams."

"I'm not signing this. That's my baby, correct?" I start to maneuver myself around the bed, trying to get to the edge. I feel the pull of the IV and other monitoring equipment across my body. "Get me the fuck out of here, Noah. Right now."

"Yes, Rylee's baby is yours, but she has also included consent to DNA testing if you want proof."

"I want to fucking talk to her. Now. I want to know why I have to file these papers if we are getting married. I want to know what the fuck is going on." I rip my hand through my hair and give all of the men standing around me a death glare.

"Mr. Warren, we need you to calm down," a nurse says as she enters the room. She walks over and pushes the guys back.

"Get me the fuck out of this bed, now," I growl at her.

"I'm sorry, sir, but I can't do that. Just relax." I watch as she reaches down and pushes the button on my morphine pump. My eyes flare wide knowing what she just did. I try to fight it but the warmth of the medicine seeps into my body.

Peace doesn't reach my brain, though. I know when I wake up Rylee will be gone, and it will be too late.

"Why?"

"It's for the best, Linc. Give her time," Noah says as he steps close to the side of the bed. My eyes fall closed.

ॐ

RYLEE

I look over at Kenzie. The tall blonde arrived with Noah this morning and has been trying to keep me distracted. I know she's also keeping an eye on me so I don't take off, but that's going to change soon. Dr. Tanner came in to tell me I need to continue bed rest until my appointment next week. He is also referring me to a dietitian after failing the glucose test. They will help me with diet to control my blood sugar so I don't have to go on medications. I also have to monitor my blood pressure. He's concerned with how high it shot up yesterday.

"I know everything is confusing right now, but Linc is a really nice guy," Kenzie says softly as she stands and stretches her body. I notice her left leg drags slightly when she walks across the room.

"Can I ask you a question?" I slide up in the bed. I'm now dressed in a pair of jeans rolled at the cuff and a blue polka-dot shirt that wraps and ties over my belly. Ollie brought me fresh clothes and my makeup bag. My hair is in a braid down my back to control my crazy curls, and the front of my hair is in a victory roll. Ollie insisted I wear ballet flats after fainting yesterday.

"Of course." Kenzie turns toward me. Her flowy peach colored baggy shirt is belted over her belly and her black leggings make her long legs look even longer. She's twenty-five weeks pregnant and her belly is only a bit bigger than mine. I must be carrying a baby elephant instead of a human with as big as I am.

"I'm a physical therapist and noticed you have a slight drop on your left side. Is it neurological or structural?"

"Oh, that." She looks down a bit flustered.

"I'm sorry."

"No, it's okay. It's just hard getting used to it. I'm a bit tired, which is when it happens. The baby kept me up last night kicking my bladder. I swear I have a soccer player in here. I was attacked almost six months ago and suffered some traumatic brain damage. The doctors said this will happen."

"I could help you, if you want."

"With?"

"Well, I can teach you exercises that will help build your endurance and teach you how to control when it happens."

"Really?"

"Yeah. I don't just do sports injuries. I did a rotation in a neurological ward and helped teach and develop some measures."

"That would be perfect. I have my dog trained to help me when I'm fatigued. But times like now when I can't have him with me would be amazing."

"It's a date. After I get off bed rest, you can meet me at my place, or I can come to yours. I can also help you make your home more efficient for you and your condition. With the baby coming, you'll need all the help you can get."

"That's for sure. This little bundle has been a complete surprise to us."

"Do you know what you're having?"

"No, we decided to wait and be surprised. My momma

and mother-in-law are throwing us a baby shower after the baby comes. Although they keep dropping stuff off."

A pang zings through my heart at the fact my mom would be concerned but happy for me. She wanted more children, but they could only have me. It was actually the only argument I ever heard my parents have. I still remember it even though I was only nine or ten at the time. My dad had wanted her to take time off to have a baby and she didn't because she said it was too late, she was too old. He suggested adoption but she said her practice was just starting to make a name for itself. She begged him to take time off and be a stay-at-home dad, but he refused. They were both so dedicated to their practices. But I know now that she was retired, she would have spoiled my baby. I rub my hand absently across my belly.

"How does your mom feel about you moving so far away while you're pregnant?" Kenzie's question causes another sharp pang.

"My parents died nine months ago."

"Oh, I'm so sorry. Noah didn't tell me."

"It's okay, I'm still processing. But that's why I moved here, too many memories."

"Can I ask how?"

"Home invasion." I give her the standard lie I give everyone.

"So you have no one but Linc's parents?"

"I don't know them. I have Ollie and Paul. They are my family."

"Linc's mom should be here any day now. They live up north in Lake Placid. You'll love her, she's really sweet. She was a schoolteacher for years until she retired to work at the shop with his dad. I'm surprised she isn't here already, but

Noah said she was waiting to see how long Linc was going to be in the hospital."

"That's nice." I avoid her eyes and look at my phone as I try to calculate how much longer I'm going to have to stay here. She's really sweet and I want to get to know her, but Ollie should have given Linc the paperwork already. I'll never get to know his parents or friends.

"Are you really okay?" she asks me as she touches my hand. "I know you and Linc are still new but you're getting married and having a baby."

"We aren't getting married."

She chuckles. "Are you sure Linc knows that? According to Noah, he claimed you for everyone to hear last night in the ER. Linc doesn't say anything unless he means it. He and I didn't get along in the beginning, but he's really a solid guy. His little girl, Samantha, is so sweet. She'll be excited to be a big sister. Her mom won't have any more kids because they'll ruin her figure. Now, that bitch is a piece of work."

"I've met Tracy, twice now, and both times she's insulted me. I saw Samantha at your wedding. She looks more like Linc than Tracy. I don't want to marry him just because I'm pregnant. I have enough money to take care of the baby and myself."

"It's not about money, and Linc wouldn't have said it just because you're pregnant. He's been talking to Noah a lot about you."

"Well, Tracy won't allow him to marry me or claim this baby." I rub my stomach again.

"Holy hell, batman," Ollie exclaims from the doorway. "Oops, sorry. I'm Ollie, her bestie." He points to me as he reaches for Kenzie's hand. "I'm the pretty one."

"I'm Kenzie, Noah's wife."

"You lucky, lucky girl. He's one fine piece of male specimen."

"Hey, I heard that," Paul grumbles as he walks in. "Leelee, you're looking beautiful. I was going to step out into the hallway and check out your security guard while my fiancé discusses what happened with Linc. Mrs. Caine, would you like to join me for coffee instead?" He tips his head at her. Paul is the charmer of the two, while Ollie is the jokester. "Oh my, no coffee for you." He motions at her stomach.

"I'll have a hot chocolate. Rylee, I'll be back in a few." She takes Paul's arm and he leads her out of the room.

"That bad?" I fall back against the bed worried because Ollie doesn't look happy.

"I just blindsided that poor guy because you never said anything to him. You need to stop running and talk to him."

"I can't." I huff. "He'll use that sexy mouth to kiss me and my mind will go to mush."

Ollie guffaws. "Seriously, there is a man out there that you can't wrap around your finger?"

"Fuck you, Ollie."

"Such a mouth, lady." His eyebrow juts up.

"I'm serious. He uses some voodoo on me and I can't tell him no. He broke my rules right from the get-go."

"And you let him?"

"Well I..." I bite my lip and avoid his eyes.

"You're in love with him." He takes my hand as he sits at my hip on the bed.

"Yeah, I'm pretty sure I am. What do I do, Ollie?"

"March up there and tell him you love him, and you were a little confused about the ex. Explain that you want to be with him." He pulls me into his arms. "Leelee, he's not going to give up. I watched him try to rip out his IV to get to you. A nurse had to come in and sedate him."

"I won't be responsible for him losing his daughter. Baby bean and I will be fine without him. Maybe I can tell him it's not his baby and to forget we saw each other."

"That doesn't sound like the brave Leelee I know."

"Well, I'm not that brave one anymore. I love that man and he's too dominant to admit that Samantha is more important than me."

"Leelee, Paul can get this figured out. Don't give up yet."

A knock on the door has both of us turning.

"Ms. Parsons, your discharge papers are ready." The day nurse hands them to me after going over the instructions. I sign them while she retrieves a wheelchair.

"Leelee, you can't just run away from this." I look over at Ollie who is standing there watching me. His expression is closed off and I know he's disappointed in me. He found love after losing my parents and his own, but I can't trust my heart. And I won't allow my child to be a pawn in Tracy's crazy control of Linc.

"I'm not running. I'm going home."

"At least let me take you up there to say goodbye to him." Ollie won't give up on me, but if I see Linc, I know I will give in to him.

"Okay, why don't you go down and hail us a cab? I'll have Ray take me upstairs." I give in and wait until he leaves the room. It's not often that I get one past Ollie, but he totally forgot we don't need a cab, Ray has a car for us.

The nurse brings in a wheelchair and I stall for a bit, giving myself time to make it seem like I went up to Linc's floor. We get on the elevator and head down to the main floor, and the door opens to Paul and Kenzie.

"I'm riding with you to your place, if that's okay. Noah will pick me up from there after he gets off."

"Perfect. You can keep an eye on Leelee." Ollie walks up

to us. "That was a fast one you just pulled on me. We'll talk about it when I get home. Paul and I are heading to the office now." He leans down to give me a kiss, and Ray heads out to get the car while Kenzie waits with me.

"I don't mind you coming over. I'm still unpacking," I answer Kenzie.

"That's okay."

When we pull up outside my new place, Kenzie gasps.

"We only live a couple miles north of you. Noah had the brownstone when we got together, and now his brother and sister-in-law live across the street from us. We can walk together once you get off bed rest, or meet at the park."

"That would be nice." I step out of the town car and across the sidewalk, then take the three steps down to my doorway. I unlock the door and disengage the alarm when we step inside. Ray heads back to the Securities International office after telling me to reengage the alarm.

"Show me to the kitchen and I'll make us some tea and we can get you resting."

"This way." I direct her. We pass both staircases, one going up to the other parts of the house, and the other heading down to the basement and access to Paul and Ollie's place. There are two ways to access the carriage house. One is across the courtyard and the other is down the hallway in the basement. We round the corner and step up into the dining room and kitchen next to the elevator. I guess I will be using it more and more due to this pregnancy.

"I like your kitchen. Very modern."

"Yeah, except it's a galley wall style, but I loved the rest of the house, so it was a sacrifice I was willing to make."

She walks over to the glass slider past the dining room and looks across the courtyard.

"You have neighbors that close? They can see right in here."

"Oh no, that's the carriage house. It's where Ollie and Paul live for now until they decide to have kids because it's only a one-bedroom. This side is a four-bedroom."

"You even have an elevator." She smiles as she waves her hand at it.

"Yep." I start the tea kettle and after it's done, we take our cups and ride the elevator up so I can show her each floor. When we get to the master floor, I excuse myself and step into the bathroom to change into a pair of flowered lounge pants and a pale pink tank top. I scrub my makeup off and pull out the braid to pile all my hair up on my head in a pineapple. When I step out, Kenzie smiles at me.

"I love to get comfy too, it's the first thing I do when I get home."

I grab my long gray-and-white striped poncho that looks like a large scarf with sleeves and slip it on.

"Do you work?"

"I used to be an emergency dispatcher, but between the leg and my hand, I can't do it anymore. Plus with the baby coming, Noah is a big bundle of nerves. I can't even make dinner without him going crazy. I crave Italian food like it's going out of style. Thank goodness his uncle Romeo owns a restaurant close by and he'll deliver to me."

"Oh, man, that sounds so good."

"Want me to order us some food?"

"Sure, let me grab my credit card."

"Oh, no, Uncle Romeo won't let us pay. What sounds good?"

"All of it." I laugh because I feel like I haven't eaten in days.

"I got it." She pulls out her cell phone and places the order.

We settle in the great room and chat, getting to know each other. I really do like her and hope we can still be friends during all this. After about thirty minutes, the bell rings and I make my way over to the security panel where I see an older man on the camera. His longish dark hair is brushed away from his face.

"Oh, that's Uncle Romeo."

I press the button. "I'll be down in a moment."

"No, I'll go get the food. You go sit in the dining room and wait for me." She orders and we both ride down the elevator together. I punch in the code on the panel so she can open the door, and she walks to the front while I go to the kitchen and get silverware and plates. I'm glad I unpacked my kitchen.

"Rylee, go have a seat," Kenzie says when she comes around the corner.

"I was getting the stuff we'll need."

"I'm sure I can find it. Have a seat, Uncle Romeo. This is Rylee, Linc's..." She pauses and looks at me. I know she's not sure how to describe our relationship.

"You'd better be his *moglie amabile*." His voice is thickly accented and I'm not sure what he called me. I cock my head and look past him to Kenzie, hoping she'll explain.

"Uncle Romeo, she's not his lovely wife." She smiles at me. "She's his fiancée."

"No, I'm not." I quickly interject.

"Well, *bellissima,* you can be my *moglie* if you need a *piccolo papa.*" He takes my hand and kisses the back of it.

"Stop flirting with her, Uncle Romeo, you know Linc will kick your ass. He's not afraid of you like Noah and the boys are." Kenzie walks over with plates and silverware and bottles of water.

"I hope you don't mind me stopping by and having a bite with you, *donne adorabili*." He sits in the chair between Kenzie and me.

"I don't mind. I just moved here from L.A. and my room-mates are still at the office." I wave behind me to their house.

We have a fun, talkative meal. Romeo tells me to call him whenever I have cravings and he'll hook me up. I haven't laughed this much in a long time. Finally, after he leaves, I start to feel tired and see Kenzie yawn too. I'm about to offer her the spare room for a nap when Noah arrives.

I stay seated and Kenzie goes to let him in. After Romeo left, I set her up a code on the panel so that she could operate it too.

"I see you called Uncle Romeo." Noah chuckles when he steps into the dining room.

"I'm so stuffed." I rub my belly.

"Yeah, he's good about that. Kenzie has a soft spot for his lasagna."

"I saw that. She wouldn't even share with me when I asked for a bite."

He takes a seat and pulls his tie loose. His hands fold on the table and I know I'm not going to like what he has to say.

"You need to talk to Linc, Rylee. He's confused and upset. Now's not the time to upset him, as you know."

"I do." I nod.

"He cares about you. He wants what is best for you and your baby."

"I don't doubt that. But, Noah, it's between us. And honestly, I want to marry for love, not because I made a mistake during a weekend fling."

"But you love him," Kenzie says, and I look at her. I can't deny what she's saying.

"Is that enough for a marriage, though? One person loving the other?"

"Maybe he loves you too." Kenzie tries to be the romantic.

"Yeah, maybe. Okay, why don't you two take off. I'm going to take a bath before I climb into bed and fall asleep."

"I'll come back tomorrow, and if you want, I'll go with you on Friday to your appointment."

"I don't want to be a burden. I'll catch a cab or an Uber."

"Ray will be back in the morning. I'm working with Ollie to get your system hooked to the S.I. one so we can be alerted if you need anything."

"I don't need security. Whoever killed my parents isn't going to follow me across the country when it was just a random home invasion."

"You and I both know that isn't true. When you're up to it, we'll be having a conversation about your parents' case. I also had my hacker get the info on your previous phones. I know what was happening."

I pause, trying to find the anger, but I know Ollie probably gave him permission to do that, and because he's my POA, he can do that. I nod at him and watch as they walk out. I arm the system again and make my way upstairs, doing exactly what I told them I would do.

Linc

CHAPTER
10

I come awake again alone. Every time I wake up, I'm alone. My mother should be here sometime today but my heart hurts because Rylee isn't here. Noah assured me via phone that he had eyes on Rylee, and she was safe and taking care of herself and the baby. He said Kenzie and Rylee were hanging out. I'm pissed after she snuck out on me and sent her attorney to see me. I look at the breakfast tray they brought in a bit ago and decide I better eat. I take a bite and instantly hate the dry eggs.

"I brought you a breakfast of champions," Noah says as he enters my room in jeans and a sweater under his jacket.

"No work today?"

"Took the day off. Kenzie has an appointment and then we have plans." He doesn't elaborate and I'm glad because I don't want to hear how good his relationship is going.

"Knock, knock," a deep voice says from the doorway, and in walks the police commissioner. At six foot four, he's taller than me and the same height as his nephew Noah. You can see the family resemblance between the two men in the jawline and eye color. "How are you doing today, Lincoln?" His voice booms when he talks.

"I'm getting better. I should be discharged tomorrow, and my mom will be here today."

"I'm picking her up from the station at three," Noah says.

"I wanted to talk to you before IA arrives. I want clarification because you're family."

"Sir, I did nothing wrong. I protected my partner and can account for the one bullet I shot." He leans forward and I see the furrow in his brow. There is something more going on than I know.

"Should I step outside since I'm not NYPD anymore?" Noah asks.

"Noah, son, you can stick around. It's because you're not

NYPD that I'm going to say this in front of you. Lincoln, know your story before you tell it. Be sure of your account of sequences because CSI findings conflict with what your partner claims happened. If you want to call a union rep, you can. I can't be in here, but I got your back. I agree with the findings and with what I believe in my gut happened."

My stomach flops with worry. Why would Rocco claim something else?

"Sir, I don't know—"

"Let's pretend I'm not the commissioner right now. I'm your uncle just as much as I'm his." He tilts his head toward Noah. "You're family, Lincoln." I nod at him and he stands to take off his long black trench coat. His three-piece tailored black suit beneath the coat is a standard for him. He unbuttons the double breast and sits back down, then leans back stretching his long legs out in front of him and crossing them at the ankles. He's trying to be relaxed but I can tell his body is coiled and ready to jump up if necessary. "Noah, man the door." He orders. Noah walks over and puts his back to the door, blocking everyone out.

"Rocco and I pulled up to the scene and I told him we needed to call for backup. He was already out of the car and said we didn't need it. I grabbed the handheld and followed him up. Rocco made first contact, identifying us to the suspect, who yelled back he was leaving in a body bag." I avoid trying to make Rocco look worse; he's my partner and you just don't do that. "I proceeded to try to talk the suspect down, but he wasn't going to have it. My partner broke down the door, and in the process, I noticed the suspect was ready to shoot, so I dove for my partner and we landed on the floor. I didn't know I had been shot at that time. I saw the suspect pop up from his hiding spot. I took a shot and hit him in the left clavicle, about the same spot he shot me. I guess he was still engaged, and Rocco determined the necessity for deadly force and took a head shot. Things are a bit fuzzy at that point."

"That's your story?"

I look at him confused, my eyebrows almost in my hairline. I look at Noah, who drops his eyes and shifts from foot to foot. "What is going on?"

"Lincoln, tell your story just like that to IAD when they get here. Don't make any rash decisions while you're on leave. Congratulations on the engagement and the new baby. I'm going to leave now." He takes my right hand and shakes it, then he moves to Noah at the door. The commissioner gives him a hug and briefly talks to him while I wonder about what's going on.

"Get a union rep, Linc, or let me get you an attorney," Noah says after his uncle leaves.

"Why? I did everything I was supposed to. What is going on?"

"I need to head back to the office, I have my new tech guy running some information for me. I'll be back with your mom at four. If IAD comes in, ask for a union rep and tell the story just like that."

"It's not a fucking story, Noah, that's what happened."

"Yeah, I and Jeremiah know that, and that's what's important." He turns and walks out.

I let my head fall back and think over everything that happened. I remember everything. I remember the pain of the bullet once I realized I was hit. Mostly I remember Rylee's face when she saw I was hurt. My reaction when Rocco held her in his arms.

Tracy had fucked me over royally between sleeping with her attorney and then suing me for complete custody and the max for child support. Her husband, Drew, was a junior partner when they met, and they got together before our separation. I knew she was cheating on me, but I was so focused on my job and avoiding her. I unwittingly was avoiding my daughter and Tracy used that against me. I've tried to make Samantha my priority over the last few years. I've taken her more times than what I'm supposed to because Tracy and Drew have a busy social life. Samantha has told me numerous times that she's heard Drew say he didn't want kids. But Tracy knows if I take her back to court and get more custody, she loses her child support. I wonder how they afford the penthouse condo they have. Drew is still a junior partner, which is basically a salaried employee. The fact that Noah suspects Tracy is sleeping with Rocco makes no sense. What does she gain from it? Tracy uses sex to advance herself. What could Rocco give her? I shake my head and try to think of something else to not give my ex-wife any more of my head space.

Several hours later I've spoken to internal affairs with a union rep present and gone through my second day of hand physical therapy. I hear voices in the hall and smile when the door pushes open and my mother stands there. She doesn't look like she's in her early sixties. Her sandy blond hair only has a little bit of gray in it. Her skin is almost flawless and she's still slender.

"Well, you just couldn't wait for Christmas to see me, you had to go and get yourself shot so I'd have to visit." She shakes her head and makes her way over to me. She's in black slacks and a white blouse with a long wool double-breasted black jacket over her arm.

"Hey, Mama." I smile and lean forward so I can kiss her cheek. At five foot three, she is about the same height as Rylee or a little shorter.

"Your dad will be down for Christmas, but we are going

to get a hotel room. I don't want to inconvenience you, and I know you get Samantha this year."

"Mom, I don't want you to stay in a hotel."

"It's only while your father is here. I'll stay at your place on the sofa until then. I can't wait to see my sweet baby girl. Now let me look at you." She takes a moment to take me in and shakes her head. "Why did you have to jump in front of that bullet? Noah won't tell me, but I know you. You pushed someone else away and took it, didn't you, kiddo?"

"Mama." I try to soothe her worries; she hates that I'm a cop.

"Why can't you go work with Noah? He doesn't get shot at."

"Um, Mama Berni, I get shot at, just not as much."

"See, there you go. Go work with him."

"Mama, we aren't fighting about this now."

"Fine. Noah promised me Uncle Romeo's cooking and he called an order in. I can't wait until he goes to get it. We got you some pasta and chicken with butter sauce so it doesn't upset your stomach." She walks over and sets her coat and purse down by the window and starts rolling up her sleeves.

"I knew coming to deliver myself again would be a good idea," Romeo says from the doorway. "I couldn't believe it when I saw Kenzie and Rylee yesterday that you had been shot—"

"You saw Ry yesterday?" I interrupt him.

"Yes. Kenzie called and asked for a super pregnancy order for her and that *bella fidanzata* of yours. She's very pretty, you did good this time around. I can see how caring she is. She's going to make a *bella mamma*." He doesn't realize the bomb he's dropped into this room.

"Lincoln Jacob Warren, you're engaged and she's expecting, and you didn't tell me?" My mom raises her voice to the decibel she used to use with her fourth graders when they got out of hand.

"Mama, I just found out Rylee was pregnant, and I told her we are getting married. She is still adjusting to it."

"Lincoln, not again. I can't watch you go through another marriage that's based only on a child. You need to find love. You need a woman who will love you like I love your father. Then maybe you'll stop jumping in front of bullets."

"Mama, Rylee is different. Before I knew she was pregnant, I was going to ask her to be mine. Now it just means more."

"Really? How long have you two been seeing each other?"

"Well, um. Let's eat dinner and then I'll discuss that with you."

"Well, *idiota,* if you don't want her, I wouldn't kick her out. She's a *bella,*" Romeo says breaking the tension. I look at him, my eyebrows dropping. If I had a gun in my hand right now, it would be pointed at him. She's mine and I won't share her or allow another man to claim her.

"That's all Uncle needed to see. Go claim your *bella*, boy, before someone else tries." Romeo walks out after hugging Noah, leaving me to get my emotions in check. The pain meds are making me angrier than normal. I take a deep breath and look at my mom.

"Mama, Rylee and I met the weekend of Noah's wedding. We haven't known each other long, but she just moved here from out west and I really care about her. Yes, it was an accident getting her pregnant, but this time it was an accident I perpetrated."

"Are you saying that you never intended to get Tracy pregnant, but you did Rylee?"

"Yeah. I was using condoms and being careful when Tracy got pregnant. I know Samantha is mine because I had DNA tests done after Tracy tried to claim she wasn't during the divorce. I knew she was mine without them, though. As for Rylee, I wanted to keep her. I still do. I want her." My head falls back.

"Well, then you better get better so you can go after her," my mom says as she pats my right hand.

We have dinner and I end up falling asleep on them before they leave. When I wake up in the middle of the night, I swear I smell Rylee's perfume in the room. I buzz the nurse and she confirms Rylee was there watching me sleep. My girl isn't going to stay away from me anymore. I'm getting her and my baby back.

§

RYLEE

It's been over a week since Linc was shot. Today is my appointment with my OB-GYN, but Veronica from the office asked if I could stop by. My blood pressure has been normal, and my blood sugar has been good too. I check my sugar after I eat and first thing in the morning. I didn't think it would be too much on me.

My hair is down in curls down my back with the sides pinned back and the front in a victory roll. I'm in a black dress with white polka dots that ends just above my knees. The bodice has a boat neckline that flows down over my bump. I'll be able to wear this when I get bigger. The skirt is round and flares out if I spin around. I've paired it with a black-and-white boucle maternity coat and my pink round toe chunky bow platforms with a buckle at my ankle. I'm not giving up my heels until I can't wear them at all.

I make my way out to the curb where Ray waits in the town car for me. I slide into the backseat and let him know where we are headed. When we pull up, I slip out and walk into the practice and head for Veronica's office. I don't know why I had to come in, but I don't want to be on her bad side more than I already am.

I knock at her door before entering. She's in a miniskirt dress with a jacket over it and heels. She's taller than me by only a couple inches, but with my tall heels we're the same height. Her dark brown hair is cropped at her shoulders in a one-length bob and her dark brown eyes are heavily lined. She had accused me of being a distraction during my interview but it's quite obvious she's on the hunt for a man with her appearance.

"Rylee, Dr. Overmyer wanted you to check out your office and he wanted me to get you the application for the day care that is on the main floor." The sound of her nasally voice almost makes me shiver.

"Thank you, Veronica."

She leads me across the floor where patients are working out with physical therapists. We enter a corner office with creamy white walls. The color is soothing instead of stark. The white desk with a slight red trim sits off to the side and has two chairs in front of it. The desk chair looks like a space chair but also comfy. The surrounding cabinet is tan and offsets the white. There are pictures on the wall of flowered fields along with some of the local sports teams and a CT of a brain. My name is on the door and I can't keep the smile from my face. I have an office, not a corner of a workout room.

"I love it." I turn to Veronica and notice she isn't paying

attention to me; she's focused on the workout floor where Lincoln is being led in by a male trainer. A woman just shorter than me with blond hair and his smile is standing with him. They get him seated on a table and start removing his sling. I know why she's focused on him, because I can't take my eyes off him either. He's sexy. His hair is mussed up and he's growing out his stubble into an actual beard now. He smiles at something the woman says and my heart stops. I'm going to have to walk right past him to get out of here and he'll see me.

"Are you done?" Veronica's voice breaks through my thoughts.

"Uh, yeah."

She hands me a file and I watch as she walks over to Linc and puts her hand on his good shoulder. She's fully flirting with him and he's just looking at her. My heart twists with jealousy and fear that she's the kind of woman he wants. Maybe he's distracted by her and won't see me. I try to slip past them, putting equipment and other patients between me and him.

"Ry. Rylee, is that you?" His voice lets me know I didn't hide well enough.

I turn and paste on a fake smile, glad I have my red lipstick on nice and bright. No one will be able to tell.

"Lincoln, what are you doing here?" My voice sounds too cheerful. Too bright.

"Rylee?" Now he's looking at me more intensely.

I walk over to him and try to fake it until I can get away. I look at my phone in the palm of my hand. I have the perfect excuse.

"Hello, Linc," I say again as I step up to him. I turn to the beautiful woman with him and reach out my hand. "Hello, I'm Rylee."

"I'm Berni, Lincoln's mother."

"Nice to meet you."

"What are you doing here?" he asks, and I remember that he was unconscious when we discussed him coming here with the doctor.

"Ms. Parsons is a physical therapist here. She starts in January." Veronica explains for me.

"You're why I'm here?" His voice is gruff and my eyes flash to his. I know that tone.

I bite my top lip and nod my head.

"How do you know Ms. Parsons?" Veronica interrupts our staring contest.

"Rylee is my fiancée and the mother of my baby." Linc doesn't even look at her. His eyes are focused on me, daring me to deny him. Deny the truth.

"Then why didn't you know she works here?" Again, Veronica interrupts.

"Miss, can we give my son and Rylee a moment?" Berni steps around me and takes Veronica's arm and leads her away.

"I have to go, Linc, I have an appointment." I start to turn but his good hand flies out and grabs my arm.

"Don't leave. I want to go with you. We need to talk. I'm worried about you and the little one. Please, Ry," he begs, and my insides turn to mush. I can't deny him. I've never been able to. I nod.

"Mom, reschedule, we are going with Ry to her appointment."

The trainer looks at me and smiles. "I have an opening this afternoon if you want to come back." He offers.

"That will work. Get this shit back on me so we can go."

I stand back and watch as they slip the sling with a pillow against his chest back on.

"I want you to squeeze this ball off and on while you are gone until you come back. See if you can get a hundred of them," the trainer says as he hands Linc a black strength ball.

"I'll make sure he does it." I purse my lips together trying not to smile.

"Thanks, Rylee," the trainer says and walks off.

I lead Linc and his mother through the building and out to the car where Ray is waiting for me. I slip the folder with the day care application into my bag and Linc settles himself next to me with his mother on my other side.

"Do you know what you are having yet?" Berni asks me as she takes in my small belly. "How far along are you?"

"I don't know." I look over at Linc and drop my eyes. "I was waiting to find out. I'm only sixteen weeks but I'm measuring at over twenty weeks."

"Lincoln was a big baby too." She laughs and then turns to look out the window.

Linc gets out when we pull up in front of my doctor's office and comes around to help me out of the car.

"Baby, those shoes are sexy, but should you be wearing them after you fainted twice?"

"Linc, you can't dictate my wardrobe. I'm feeling fine, and until I feel uncomfortable in them, I will wear them." I walk past him to the door and start to pull it open.

"Ry, I might be down an arm but I'm still your man and can open doors and take care of you," Linc growls as he leans over me, taking the door from my hand.

His mother stands there taking us in. She hasn't said anything more to me and I'm getting nervous that she doesn't like me, but it doesn't matter because I can't be with him.

"Rylee." I look up to see Kenzie waiting in the lobby.

"Hello." I wave to Linc and his mom. "I ran into them at the office. He insisted on coming along."

"Perfect. Berni and I can wait in the waiting room for you." Kenzie offers and I smile as I walk to the reception desk to check in.

After all my paperwork is filled out, they call my name and I get up expecting Linc to follow right along, but he stays seated. I stop and turn toward him. His head is dropped and his body is tight.

"Would you like to come with me?" I ask to put him at ease.

"Yes." His smile is blinding, and this is the reason I can't tell him no.

He follows along and the nurse shows us to a room.

"Ms. Parsons, you'll find the cups in the restroom to give us a urine sample. Then I will get your weight and check your blood sugar." She looks down at my shoes. "Without those please." I nod and set down my stuff on one of the chairs. I also send her a copy of my past blood sugar readings from the app on my phone so she will have them in my file.

After she takes my vitals and I give her a urine sample, I return to the room and sit on the table with my feet dangling, waiting for Dr. Tanner to walk in.

"Thank you for letting me be a part of this." Linc's voice is quiet.

"You're the baby's father." I pull my top lip into my mouth trying not to say more.

"I want to be a part of this baby's life. With my new attorney, I'm going to fight Tracy. She can't keep Samantha away from me just because of us. I want to be a part of your life, Ry." He stands up and walks toward me. He places his right hand along my neck and tips my chin up with his thumb so I can look into his eyes. "Please give me a chance."

"Linc—"

"Now this looks more like the man you would have chosen." Dr. Tanner walks into the room. "I'm Dr. Tanner. I'm an old friend of Clarice." He turns his back on Linc and walks to the counter and leans against it.

"Clarice was my mother." I clarify for Linc.

"Your blood sugar levels are looking good; the diet is working so far, but I still want to monitor your sugar closely. I see you gave us a record of your blood pressure too. Those are good for now, and today's was good when the nurse took it. You can come off bed rest, but if you have any more issues, I will put you back on it until delivery. I'll perform an ultrasound today and schedule you for another glucose study in a couple weeks. With your family history, I want to monitor it carefully. Before I start the ultrasound, do you want to find out what you are carrying?" He looks between Linc and me.

"I don't care," I tell Linc.

"Sure, why not," Linc says.

We are directed to another room. It's spacious and has a sofa and a couple chairs. I slip off my heels again and look around the room. It's less sterile with darker walls and the lights are dimmer than in the other room. The table is more padded and has pillows and a blanket.

"Do you want your mother to come in here too?"

"She would love that."

"I can go get your family, if you'd like." The nurse offers and Linc tells her that would be nice.

I climb up onto the padded table and wait with my hands twisting in my lap and biting my lip. I'm finding out what I'm carrying. I'm here with Linc, his mom, and his best friend's wife. I've never felt so alone. So lost. The overabundance of hormones rushing through my body has tears pooling in my eyes. The door opens and in walks all his support, but following behind them is the one person I've learned to count on. Ollie walks right over to me and takes my hand.

"You didn't think I'd forget about today, did you?"

I hiccup and release a sob and he pulls me into his arms. He holds me for a few moments, smoothing his hand down my back.

"May I cut in?" Linc's voice breaks through us and I look up at him. Ollie still holds me and Linc's jaw ticks slightly.

"Okay." Ollie steps back and Linc slips his one good arm around me and pulls me into him.

"Ry, I'm here for you, and you alone. I want this baby, but I want you more." His words are whispered into my ear and the tears come harder.

"What? No tears. We haven't even looked at this little munchkin. We might not be able to tell what this little one is. I mean, I can tell if it's an alien, but I might not know if it's a boy or a girl. Okay?" Dr. Tanner jokes.

"Okay," Both Linc and I say.

"Now, since you're wearing a dress, I'll have you cover your lap with a sheet and lift your dress up to just under your bra." He hands me a sheet and I slip it over my legs as I lie back and slide my dress up. Ollie stands back but is still close if I need him. Linc is standing right next to me and takes my hand in his good one. Dr. Tanner pulls out the gel and squirts some on his probe then onto my stomach. As soon as he places it on my belly, the heartbeat swooshing through the speakers around the room has the tears returning to my eyes. That's my baby. Linc's hand squeezes mine.

Dr. Tanner starts pointing out parts of the baby and taking measurements. He continues for a moment and then starts focusing on the baby's anatomy more.

"Okay, ladies and gentlemen, I present you with a little boy."

"A son? We're having a boy?" Linc's voice is gruff and he stumbles over his words for a moment. Tears are rolling down my face as I see the joy on his face. He leans over me. "Sexy, you're giving me a son. I love you." He stands back up and turns to his mom. "A son. You're getting a grandson."

My heart rate hasn't returned to normal. He told me he loved me. Does he really? Because he hasn't said it again. Ollie steps over to me and takes me in his arms, helping to get me rearranged.

"Breathe, Leelee," he says softly, and I try but I can't.

"Calm down, Rylee." Dr. Tanner steps over toward us. "Follow me." He takes a slow, big breath in and holds it, then he slowly releases it. I try but my lungs won't let me. My head is swimming. I can't focus on anyone.

"Calm down, sexy. I got you. Take a breath for me." Linc's voice breaks through everything. "Come on, sexy, another breath." I take it and look into his blue eyes. They are soft like the sky on a clear day.

I want to talk to him, but nothing comes. I just look at him, trying to tell him with my eyes everything I can't say.

"I know, baby." He nods and leans in, taking my lips gently. "I do love you. It took me all of a week to realize that if I don't have you, I have nothing, and I want it all. I want this baby, you, my daughter, and a life with you."

"I love you too, Linc," I blabber out and lean into him, trying to avoid his injured arm as much as possible. When I pull away, I realize we are alone in the room.

"Where did they all go?"

"They left to give us a moment together. I wanted to tell you over candles, flowers, or while I was deep inside you, but I couldn't hold back. I love my daughter, and now I'm going to have a son. I can't wait, baby."

"But Tracy?"

"We'll figure it out together. Okay?"

"Yes."

Rylee

CHAPTER
11

After the doctor, we all decide to get some lunch before Linc's PT appointment.

"So, for Christmas, Linc has Samantha and Ron will be coming down. Ron and I will stay at a hotel since Linc's apartment isn't big enough for all of us. Would you like to spend the holiday with us? It will be cramped but cozy," Berni asks me.

"You can all come to my place. I'm having a service come in and decorate because I can't with this." I wave my hand down to my belly. "I'm sure I can get someone to cater for us too."

"Cater? Darling, I'll make food, just show me the kitchen."

"Okay, after Linc's appointment we can all go to my place."

"I won't be home until late. I have a late meeting and Paul wants us to have dinner with his parents tonight." Ollie interjects.

"Oh, you live with Rylee?" Berni asks and I see the awkward moment starting.

"Berni, you need to see Rylee's place. She has a carriage house that Ollie and Paul live in. She has a whole house to herself."

"Well that sounds nice."

𓃹

I PUSH through the door of my house and disengage the alarm. I turn toward Linc and his mom worried they are going to hate my house. Linc walks through into the dining room and his mom follows him.

"Oh, I'm sure I can make a proper Christmas dinner in

this kitchen." Berni's voice breaks me from my fear. I turn to smile at her.

"I can show you the rest of the house now."

I proceed to show them around and even invite Berni and Ron to stay in my spare room instead of getting a hotel room. She's really nice and has done nothing to make me feel uncomfortable. When I take them to the basement and show them the large wine cellar that Ollie and Paul are trying to fill up, as well as the hallway that leads to their place, Berni laughs. She looks up at the ceiling and gasps.

"Are those sky lights in your basement?"

"Yeah, I'll show you where they are."

We head back upstairs, and I open the slider to the courtyard between Ollie's place and mine. I point out the skylights in the ground.

"That is really neat. Did you have this place built for you?"

"No, I found it when I was here back in September. I knew as soon as I saw it that it would be perfect for us. Ever since my parents died, Ollie has been overly protective, and it just got worse when I found out I was pregnant."

"Oh, your parents are gone?"

"Yes, they died several months ago."

Linc's phone rings and he steps into the house to take the call, leaving Berni and me out in the courtyard. We sit down on the outdoor furniture. It's chilly but the sun is shining bright.

"Linc didn't tell me that. Actually, he didn't tell me anything about you. It was Uncle Romeo who told me Linc was dating and expecting too."

"Oh."

"Well, obviously you didn't get pregnant thinking my son

was loaded because you most definitely have more money than him," she says as she looks around.

"Linc married Tracy because she was pregnant?" My breath stills in my lungs again.

"Oh, I thought you knew that." She turns back to me with concern in her eyes. She reaches out to take my hand. "Linc just told me last week that he used condoms all the time with Tracy and yet she still got pregnant. He said with you it was an accident, but a pleasant one because he wanted to keep you." I rear back my head and my eyes search for Linc through the glass. When he turns to face me and sees the look on my face, he says something into his phone before pocketing it and rushing out to me.

"Ry, sexy, what's the matter?" He squats down in front of me. I don't want him to fall back, so I pull at him to stand and I stand with him.

"You wanted to get me pregnant?" The words rush from my mouth. His eyes whip to his mom and back to me.

"Ry, I told you that last night we were together I wanted a chance. I wanted you. You said you were mine. After you fell asleep, I realized we hadn't used a condom. I didn't know if you were on birth control, but I wanted a baby with you. I want everything with you. As for Tracy, I used condoms, and yes, she still got pregnant. Nothing is fail proof. After we had Samantha, I started wearing them again because I suspected she was cheating. I'm fairly certain she was never faithful to me. I should have divorced her sooner than I did but I was staying for my daughter. I'll kill any man that tries to flirt or get with you. So if you don't want me to go to prison, you better be faithful. I do love you, and trust is a big part of that, and right now I know you'd never cheat on me. God, sexy, I know you're not with me for my money. I worry you're going to think I'm with you for it."

"No, Linc." I rise up on my tippy-toes and kiss his lips. His good arm wraps around me and holds me tight.

LINC

When I looked out and saw her face, I knew Mama had said something. I didn't want Rylee to doubt my love or me, ever. I told Noah I'd call him back and rushed out here to her. The words "I love you" did slip out, but they were meant to come out. I've thought of her and the baby every day since the hospital. But I had to start getting better before going after her. I didn't expect to see her, and I'm glad I did.

We have dinner together, and as the night draws closer, I don't want to leave her, but I can't push her. So, as we head out, I pull her against me again.

"Text me if you need anything."

"Okay, Linc."

"Soon we'll be together, and you won't get away from me." I grin at her and she smiles. She's so beautiful. I lean down and kiss her small stomach. "Night, son."

IN THE WEEK and a half since I started physical therapy and told Rylee how I feel, we've been together every day. She comes over to my place or I go to hers. Tomorrow is Christmas Eve and I'm on my way to get my daughter for the holiday and introduce her to Rylee. I wanted to introduce her before this, but Tracy wouldn't let me see her. Today I have Paul with me and I'm getting my daughter, no matter what.

117

We ride the elevator up to the thirteenth floor where Tracy and Drew's penthouse condo starts; it's two floors.

"Remember, don't engage her. You need to remain calm and let me be your voice." Paul's in a light blue suit today with a checkered blue vest. His thin black tie offsets all the blue. He has his winter coat folded over one arm and his briefcase in the other. In the last couple of weeks working with him, I've found he might dress over the top but he's extremely smart. He says he has a plan and not to worry, but I know Drew is extremely cunning. I just hope Paul can fight dirty in that suit.

I'm in jeans with a white button-up shirt, a gray sweater, and a black blazer. Getting my bandaged arm into this jacket sucked but I wanted to look semiprofessional if this ended up going sideways. My arm is still in the huge black brace. I have to wear it twenty-four seven until mid-January. The only time I'm allowed to take it off is for showers and therapy. Rylee has been working some massage into my therapy on my neck, back, and other shoulder. She's worried I'm going to get too stiff. I love her hands on me and can't wait until I can sink into her body again.

My dad is supposed to be getting in now too; Rylee and my mom are picking him up. I was shocked when Rylee offered my parents a place to stay for the holiday, and when she said Samantha and I could stay too, I was happy. She really did have a service come and decorate her house. The tree in her great room brushes the ceiling. This is her first holiday without her parents and she's had moments where I can see the sadness, but my mom has pulled her out of it by making cookies and helping with planning. Rylee and my mom get along better than I ever thought they would. Now I just need my dad and Samantha too as well. Because I'm marrying her sooner rather than later.

The elevator dings and the doors open, and we make our way to the door. I ring the bell and it goes off like a gong. Tracy's housekeeper answers the door. "Mr. Warren, please come in. May I take your coats?" She directs that question to Paul.

"We are good, thank you," he says to her as he tips his head. When he looks at her again and smiles, she practically melts right there. Paul even beguiles the older ladies, I see. Wait until Tracy gets a load of him, she's only met Ollie.

"Oh, hello, Lincoln, who's your friend?" Tracy steps around the corner with a brandy glass in her hand. She's dressed in a white slim skirt and a red blouse; her red heels click against the floor. Her jewelry sparkles and her blond hair is smooth and straight, her crystal blue eyes bright from the dark liner against them. Rylee is made up a lot, but she looks effortlessly beautiful compared to Tracy, who obviously had Botox recently because when she smiles at Paul nothing crinkles.

"This is my attorney, Paul Tyndale."

"Why would you bring your attorney? I thought you had that other man." Her voice has a slight catch. Catching her unprepared is perfect.

"Darling, who was at the door. Well, hello, Lincoln. Ah, Mr. Tyndale, are you representing Lincoln now?" Drew is in navy slacks; his green shirt and tie probably looked perfectly pressed earlier but now they don't. The tie is pulled loose, the top button of his shirt undone, and his sleeves are rolled up. They knew I was coming but they sure didn't expect Paul.

"Mr. Adams, nice to finally meet you in person." Paul doesn't waste a moment. "I thought I would come by with my client just in case there was something said. After the hospital incident, I don't want threats thrown around lightly."

Tracy gasps, her hand going to her chest like she's shocked. Bitch.

"Daddy," Samantha yells as she comes down the stairs. "Mother said you weren't coming today." She walks right over to me and wraps herself around my uninjured side. I lean down to kiss the top of her head.

"What were you doing upstairs, young lady?" Tracy raises her voice and I'm instantly on alert. For some reason they make Samantha sleep down on this floor instead of upstairs where there are two bedrooms besides the master. It's like Samantha is a guest and not a part of the family.

"I was taking up a basket of clothes for Eleanor," Samantha says as she points toward the laundry room where the housekeeper has gone.

"That is her job."

"I was just helping, Mother."

"Go to your room, Samantha, let us adults talk." Tracy waves her hand toward where Samantha's room is.

"Monkey, go get your bag, we are going to be leaving here in just a bit. Papa can't wait to see his girl."

"Papa and Meemaw came down?"

"Yep, now go get your bag."

"But I didn't pack, Daddy. Mother said I wasn't going."

I swing my head to Tracy, my teeth grinding but I calm myself.

"Go on, monkey." She takes off toward her room and squeals in excitement.

"Inside voice, Samantha." Drew raises his voice then turns back to us. "I've filed a motion to postpone any visitation until we get this situation figured out. According to my wife, your *friend* was rude and offensive to her. That isn't in

Samantha's best interest." Drew folds his arms over his chest but the tick in his jaw tells me he's not happy with this.

"Let's be honest here, Drew, you had reservations at The Plaza for the holiday weekend; you don't want to change those because of my daughter." It's hard to cross my arms and imitate his stance with this fucking brace.

"Your motion has been countered. I have your copy of the denial from the judge, along with our filing to pull Samantha from your care not only for the holiday but until she returns to school."

"On what grounds?" Drew spits as he rakes his hand through his hair.

"On the grounds you've denied Lincoln his visitation for the last two weeks."

"He was in the hospital and with that tramp," Tracy yells, her voice hitting a decibel dogs can hear all over the tri-state area.

"She's not a tramp, and I was out of the hospital the first week. My mom was with us and I didn't get to see my daughter. I was shot and you refused to bring her to see me," I growl.

"I told your girlfriend if you claim that baby, I was going to take Samantha away from you. Samantha is your only priority, not some bimbo's baby."

"Call her a name again, Tracy..." I step toward her.

"Did you just threaten my wife?" Drew steps between me and her.

"No, Mr. Adams, he did not threaten her, he promised that we will file a defamation suit if she doesn't change her attitude. Now." Paul interjects.

"You can't be his attorney, you're fucking her too. Both you and that other asshole live with her," Tracy yells again.

"I said watch it." I step closer, even with one arm in a brace I'm sure I can take Drew.

"I'm calling the police now." Drew pulls out his phone.

"Go right ahead, but why don't you ask your wife to call her personal police officer, seeing as they are sleeping together."

"Her what?" Drew whips his head between Paul and Tracy.

After the internal affairs detectives cleared me of the shooting, Securities International's newest computer guy found out about Rocco and Tracy's affair. Paul pulls out a file of pictures and hands them to Drew.

"You're fucking another cop. You told me Lincoln was a mistake. But now you're sleeping with this guy?" He holds up a picture of Tracy and Rocco embracing before they step onto the elevator at a hotel.

"It's just a fling so I could get information on Linc so I can keep my daughter. He means nothing."

"Your daughter," he yells. "Your daughter that you don't want around here. The one you want to send to boarding school." His voice rises louder and his body locks up tighter practically vibrating from his anger. He pulls out another picture. "This is my fucking boss!" He throws the picture at her.

"Oh, yeah, that one is your boss. She's sleeping with him to find out information about the sale of Warren Sports. She wants her daughter to inherit money in the sale." I turn to look at Paul. My parents are selling the store?

"You're what?" Drew yells again and a movement off to our side catches my eye.

"Monkey, come here." I walk toward her when I see the tears rolling down her face. I don't know how much she's heard but she's upset, and I don't like that.

"Put her down. You can't take her. I need her," Tracy yells as she stumbles toward us, her drunkenness quite evident.

I push Samantha behind my legs and Tracy's body collides with mine. I grunt but the pain is moot to protecting my daughter.

"Mr. Adams, get control of your wife," Paul yells to be heard over Tracy's screaming. Tracy hits me in the shoulder but I stand my ground.

There is a pounding on the door and the housekeeper slips past us to get it. Two officers walk in and I know them. One walks over and pulls Tracy back before she hits me again.

"What's going on here?" the other officer asks.

"He's trying to kidnap my daughter," Tracy screams.

"Sir, I'm Detective Warren's attorney and it's his visitation. Here is the paperwork." Paul hands him a copy. "I'd like Mrs. Adams charged with assaulting my client." Paul doesn't pause. "Come on, Linc and Samantha." He holds out his arm to direct us toward the door. His body is between Tracy and us. She charges him, but he keeps her back.

"Drew, do something, he's taking my baby."

"No. I quit. I will be filing for divorce after the holiday weekend. Officers, take her away, I saw her assault him." Drew turns his back and walks to the bar where he pours himself several fingers of something from a glass decanter.

"You can't do this to me. Lincoln, if you let them do this, you'll be sorry," Tracy screams and I'm already sorry that I let this go on for as long as I have.

"Detective Warren?" The officers look at me. I don't want my daughter to see this, but it's time Tracy got a taste of her own medicine.

"Please wait until I have my daughter out of sight." I walk with Samantha to the elevator and Paul steps in beside us.

As the doors close, I turn my baby girl to face me so she doesn't see her mother get put in cuffs. Tracy continues to scream, threatening everyone with legal action and then bodily harm. I ignore her and hold my daughter to me.

"Daddy, what's happening to Mother?" I hate that Tracy makes her call her that. "Do I have to come back here?"

"Monkey, don't worry about your mom right now. She is upset and the officers are going to help her calm down. As for coming back, not for a while."

"How about we talk once we get Samantha settled at Leelee's?" Paul brushes his hand through his hair, pushing it back.

"Yeah." I can't believe any of what just happened. I knew about Rocco but had no clue why she was doing it. But fucking Drew's boss, one of the senior partners, so that she could keep an eye on my parents' sale... That shocks me. The fact she was going to send my daughter to boarding school is another thing I didn't know about.

"But, Dad, I'm supposed to go away to school in January." Samantha looks up at me.

"No, you're not. You're staying at your school you're in right now."

"I can't, Mother withdrew me Friday."

My jaw locks and I look over to Paul.

"I'll take care of it."

When the town car pulls up outside Rylee's, I pray she's doing better than I am. I can feel wetness on my arm and worry that Tracy busted my stitches. I try not to look so that Samantha doesn't worry. Paul can't call the school until after break, but Tracy shouldn't have been able to withdraw her without me knowing about it.

"Where are we?" Samantha asks.

"This is my girlfriend's place; she and I are getting ready

to move in together and get married. I wanted you to meet her. We are having Christmas here."

"You have a new girlfriend? I thought you said your girlfriend lived in California."

"She did. She moved here."

"Come on, kiddo, Leelee is excited to meet you. She and your grandma went and got stuff to fix up a bedroom for you."

"I'm moving in here?"

"Only if you want?" I'm honest with her. If she's not ready, we'll take it slow for her too. My girls and son are my world.

The door opens and I step into chaos.

Rylee

CHAPTER
12

Getting to know Berni has been a lot of fun. Every time I start to think of my parents and start missing them, Berni distracts me. For the last two days, we've been setting up Samantha's bedroom on the floor below the master. I found out her favorite color isn't pink but purple, and she loves to read and dance. I also found out she likes unicorns. I hope she likes the room I set up facing the city instead of the courtyard. I offered to let Linc and Samantha stay here over the holiday while Berni and Ron were here, but I don't want her to feel like she has to.

Berni has also helped with setting up the nursery. Linc wanted a blue and green color theme. We both agreed dinosaurs would be a cute addition. The only disagreement we've had is me buying everything. But I have the money and we've talked about how much he spends for Samantha to go to a private school, on top of his child support. Tracy insists on Samantha going to the school but won't help pay for it. It's a really good school and I understand getting into a school this good is hard, but I want our son to have just as much if not more than Samantha, and with Linc insisting he pay for everything, I know that won't happen. Every time he gives me money, I put it into an account that I will somehow figure out how to get back to him. I know it's deception but I can't stand the thought of him struggling. Linc is a proud man. A man that I've found I'm falling more in love with every day.

Linc is on his way to get Samantha for our holiday together, while Ray drives Berni and me to the train station to pick up Ron. Tracy hasn't been very supportive of our relationship. I'm worried she is going to make it more difficult on Linc. Ollie is at the office in case Paul needs him to do any emergency filings. I'm willing to back away until everything is settled if that's what I have to do, but Linc won't let me do that. I rub my hand down my belly and look across the busy train station. Berni is standing next to me in her black winter coat that reminds me of a classic military style trench coat. She's in black low-heeled boots with jeans and a colorful blouse. Her long blond hair is pulled back into a smooth ponytail. I'm in maternity jeans and a white shirt with a plaid shirt tied over the top of my little bump. My hair is all up in a bun with a red bandanna in my hair and my signature victory roll. I have on a black maternity Verity boucle coat buttoned over my bump. Linc has been harping on me about the heels, so to make him feel better and because it snowed, I'm wearing a pair of lower heeled retro Victorian boots in black with buttons up the side. My jeans are rolled just enough to show them off.

I told Ray to stay with the car so he didn't have to fully park. Berni and I are standing here waiting, and I watch as a tall man with brown hair that has gray spread through it walks toward us. His face is lined with wrinkles and he's smiling at Berni, but his smile falters when he looks at me. Oh man, do I look bad? I start to look down when an arm wraps around my upper body and a hand goes across my throat. I try to jerk away but the person pulls me back into their body and something presses into my side. I look down at the gun aimed at my baby and my heart stops. Berni turns to look at me as I'm being pulled away.

"Hey, what are you doing?" Berni yells and police around the station start to converge on us.

"Stay back. I'll kill the baby and her," a voice I recognize but can't place says from behind me. I try to turn my head so I can see him, but his hand tightens across my throat, squeezing tightly.

"Please don't do—" He squeezes again and I struggle for air.

"Stand back," he yells at the cops, and people start to scream and run as he waves around the gun.

He drags me back but not toward the doors where Ray could help me. A crowd of people coming off the train scurry and we blend in with them. I can't see Berni or Ron anymore, and the cops can't see us. I'm pushed through a door into an alleyway. I fight my eyes closing from the lack of oxygen and try to keep myself calm for the baby. I'll fight to get away from whoever this is. I know what he's done in the past. I know my life could be over if I'm not careful. I'm shoved face-first into the back of a van. I use my hands to keep from falling on my belly. The doors are slammed shut behind me and I turn to look around. The windows at the back are painted black and I'm in the dark. I hear a door open in the front, but I can't see anything, there is a black wall there too. I rummage through my purse and pull out my cell phone. I dial Linc but it goes straight to voicemail. I dial Noah.

"Help me," I whisper into the phone.

"Fuck." Noah's voice is loud, and I turn down my volume.

"Stop talking, bitch," is bellowed from the front and the wall vibrates as if he hit it. He slams on the brakes and the van lurches back hard. I scream as I fall backward. The phone flies from my hand and it's too dark to see where it went. I just pray it stayed connected.

I dump my purse and search it in the dark, feeling each of the items. I find a pen and slip it into my coat pocket. Next I come up with my car keys, and finally I feel a TheraBand Linc put in my purse yesterday after physical therapy. I twist it around my hand and think about how I can use it. I'm going to fight with everything I have. I take off my boots and break the heels off them. I can throw them or stab with them. I slip those into my other pocket then put my boots back on.

I sit against the back wall of the van in the corner and wait. I'm only going to have one chance and surprise is one of the things in my favor. Whoever this is isn't going to expect me to come out swinging or even wanting to fight. They know I'm pregnant, but what they don't know is I'm a momma grizzly when it comes to my baby. I'll kill them before I let them hurt me or my baby.

I listen to the sound the tires make, trying to place where we are heading. I know when we get on one of the bridges and when we come off it. I continue to sit there reserving my energy for the fight ahead. When my stomach growls, I reach over in the dark and feel around for the protein bar I had in my bag. I munch on it and take small sips from the water bottle. Ollie always teases me about how big my purse is, now I have proof that carrying the big bag has advantages.

The sound of the road changes. We're driving over gravel now. The van lurches to a stop and I move to the side of the doors that open out. I wrap the TheraBand around each hand and press my back into the side of the van, making myself not only small but giving me the advantage.

The doors swing open one at a time and I patiently wait, praying my attacker tries to step in so I can wrap the band around their neck. I'd squeeze until they let me go.

"Come out here, bitch." A baseball bat is swung into the darkness. "If I come in, you'll regret it." The voice niggles at a memory. I know it but can't place it.

I don't say anything when the bat is pushed toward me. I

wrap the band around the end and yank, but the man is stronger and fights me too. My body is thrown around, but I yank harder. When he lets it go, I fall back and it rolls out of my hands. I scramble to get up, but he grabs my booted foot. I kick out at him, screaming and hoping we aren't as alone as it seems. He pulls me and I feel around for the bat. My fingertips wrap around the handle and I come up swinging. I don't even look where I'm aiming, I just swing and feel when it connects with him.

"You fucking bitch." The man falls back and I scoot out of the van.

I swing again, remembering all the years I helped players and hearing the batting coaches give advice. I square up and swing higher, aiming for his head. He turns and I'm shocked when I see his face but I don't stall. His green eyes flare wide and his dirty blond hair is matted to his head from the blood from my first blow. I hit him again and this time he falls to the ground. He's no longer the star baseball player, the hot guy that flirted with me to get his way. He's the man who has threatened my life. I watch him for a moment as his chest rises and falls but I wait too long because he starts to move and crawl toward the front of the van. I turn and run, keeping a hold of the bat for protection. We are in a wooded area I don't recognize. We could be anywhere with as long as he drove. I run through the trees, branches slapping my face and body. I don't care, I need to get away from him.

All the pieces fall into place. The phone calls, my parents' deaths, the threats. I was on the board of physicians that determined he wasn't eligible to play after he threw out his arm. We'd only benched him until he could recover from surgery. But he decided he wanted to play and went with a minor team without letting the owners of the team know he was doing it. He blew his shoulder completely playing in a game, and when he came back and said it was my physical therapy that did it, another player came forward with video footage of him playing. His name is Trajan. He was going to be a huge star, if he could just control his temper and learn when to listen.

"I'm going to find you and kill you," he yells and fires his gun. I start to scream but cover my mouth so he can't find me. "I killed your parents. I killed Harris. I'll kill you too, along with the other two doctors who ruined my career. You should have just let me fuck you, now I'm going to rape you and take what I want." He continues to shout. Harris was the player that showed the managers and owners the footage of Trajan playing for another team.

I keep running, praying I can put some distance between him and me. My boots slip on the snowy rock covered ground. I trip on a stick and fall forward. My hands shoot out in front of me to keep from falling on my face or the baby. I cry out as my wrist contracts in pain, the bat rolls from my grip.

"Got you." I hear him and then the brush as he moves toward me faster.

I scramble to my feet and take off into the darker part of the woods. Maybe I can find a place to hide. I spot a thick brush with a log lying on its side. I climb over the log and see a cliff heading down into a river below me. I twist to the side and skirt the edge until I find a ledge below me. I think I can carefully slide down to it and maybe hide there when I'm grabbed from behind.

"I've got you now, bitch. Want to go for a swim?" He holds me over the edge, and we struggle.

LINC

"I can't believe you fucking let her go without you and now she's been taken," I bark at Ray. "You were supposed to protect her."

"He took her in a crowded train station at gunpoint, Lincoln. Ray wouldn't have been able to do anything more than we did," my father says as he tries to calm me.

"What did the man look like?"

"You're going to think I'm crazy, but he looked like the guy from that California baseball team all the girls were freaking out about last season. The one that got benched for the remaining season during playoffs," Mom says and I look at her.

"What?"

"Wait a minute, Berni. Did he look like Trajan Miner, the pro-player," Ollie asks her, and she nods. "Oh fuck!"

"What?"

Noah comes into the room; he's been on the phone since he got a call from Rylee. She'd tried to call me, but I was dealing with Tracy at the time. My heart sunk when I stepped through the front door and found out she was missing.

"Eddie is triangulating the call before it disconnected. They were heading north on the Palisades Interstate Parkway." Noah offers but I know that without a for sure area we have nothing.

My phone rings in my pocket and I pull it out to see the local precinct number.

"Warren."

"Are you sorry now?" Tracy sneers through the phone and I clench it tightly in my hand.

"What the fuck have you done with her?" It takes everything in me not to scream and yell at her. My voice is calm, but I can hear the grit in it, and I know she'll know I'm not fucking around.

"Oh, Lincoln, I told you you'd be sorry. I met a friend of hers online when I was researching her. He's a young lover but he was thirsting for revenge. I just pointed him in the right direction." Her voice is laced with so much sugary sweetness I wonder if I'm going to need to call my dentist when we are done.

"Tracy." Noah and Paul both head in my direction. Paul tries to grab the phone, but I pull away from him. I can hear Noah on his phone talking to someone.

"Drop the charges and give me your cut of the sale of the shop and I'll tell you where he took her. But mind you, it's a big area. I can't be sure he took her right there and I can't guarantee what shape she and that bastard child will be in. He really can't wait to fuck her."

"I'll kill you," I growl. "If one hair is out of place, I'll kill you."

"Tsk, tsk. This is a recorded call."

"I know that, and you just confessed to sending a mad man after my fiancée, not to mention extortion."

"Lincoln. Lincoln. Lincoln. Haven't you learned already? I'm always several steps ahead of you." There is a shuffling across the line. "Hey, let me go. You can't do this. I'm entitled to one phone call." She screams and then another voice comes across the line.

"Detective Warren, she'll be waiting in an interrogation room for you." The line goes dead and I look over at Noah.

"I called in a favor. Let's go."

I turn to look for Samantha.

"Don't worry about her, son, we'll protect her," my dad says as he wraps his arm around my mother's shoulders.

"She's upstairs playing in her new room. You go bring my new daughter-in-law home to me." She smiles.

Ollie and Paul come with us, but Ray stays at the house to protect my family. He better not fail again, or not only will Noah fire him, I'll hurt him.

Noah jumps into the front seat of his Jeep. The memories of Noah doing this to go get his girl back are still raw and I pray we find Rylee safe.

"Get that shit out of your head," Noah says without looking at me.

"I can't lose her." I choke.

"You won't. She's not ready to give up, and you better not be either," Ollie says from the back seat, his hand lands on my good shoulder.

"Thank you." I turn to look at Noah.

"Haven't done anything yet." He dials a number through his Bluetooth and Zeke's deep voice comes across the line.

"Ready to roll?"

"We are heading to the Thirteenth Precinct where Tracy is being held. She knows where Trajan took Rylee."

"Trajan Miner? The professional baseball player that got fired has Rylee?" Zeke exclaims across the line.

"Yeah, she was on the board that said he shouldn't play anymore." Ollie supplies.

"Rylee worked for the Los Angeles Stars? That's so fucking hot." Jericho adds in.

"Jeri, do I need to remind you she's mine," I growl.

"Back off, you little fucker." A shuffling sound comes across the phone. "We'll meet you at the precinct," Zeke says and then hangs up.

❦

WE'VE BEEN ARGUING with Tracy for over thirty minutes. Rylee has been missing for over two hours now and I can feel our time running out. This is the last play we have. I walk over to the door and pull it open slightly.

"I'll do it." I look at Noah and Paul. "I'll tell Tracy I'll give her the money. Anything. I'll do anything to get Rylee back."

"You can't do that," Paul says. "She'll be able to make bail, and you don't know how much money you'll be getting."

"I'll do it," Ollie says, his head dropping. "I can give her half a million dollars right now."

"None of you are giving her any money," Jeremiah Caine says. We turn from the glass where the others have been staring at Tracy. She wants money and I don't care, I'll do whatever it takes to get Rylee back.

"I have to, Commissioner Caine."

He tips his head to the side and his look turns thoughtful. "And if she asked you to renounce that baby and leave Rylee forever?" I stand straighter.

"I'd do it if it meant Rylee and my son were safe."

"You don't know that he hasn't killed her already."

"I'll do whatever I need to." I turn and yank the door open the rest of the way.

"What do you want, Tracy? I'll give you anything you want. Just tell me where he took her."

"Anything, Lincoln?" Her smile is smug. I drop my eyes and roll my good shoulder forward in defeat.

"Anything," I mumble, praying I'm pulling this off.

"Half a million dollars and you can never see her again. Have that lawyer write it up."

"Only if she is safe."

"Of course, he's waiting for me to call him."

137

My heart seizes in my chest with the thought I won't ever be able to see Rylee again. Feel her body under or above mine. I won't get to hold my son and watch him grow. The pain is too much and I turn away trying to hold back the emotions. Giving her the show she needs.

"Paul, write it up." The words leave my lips, but I can't hear them over the silence where my heart used to beat. Everything is riding on this.

Paul writes up the affidavit. I wait until she signs it and then look at it.

"Tell me where she is, and I'll sign it." I look up from the paperwork to her. My eyes bore into hers. I wait with the pen poised over the paperwork.

Tracy looks up at the wall looking for a clock. "What time is it?"

"It's five thirty," Paul says as he looks between her and me.

"I only have thirty minutes to call him and tell him you paid, or he kills her," Tracy says and my blood runs cold. She's been playing us this whole time, trying to get us to run the clock down.

I slide my phone over to her. "Call him. I'm signing the paper now." I put the tip of the pen on the paper and wait for her to dial as she watches me, pushing the minutes down closer. I start to sign my first name.

She dials. "Hey, handsome, I told you I'd get it." There is a pause and then she smiles and looks right at me. "Tell her he sold her to you, and you do what you must with her. I'll see you soon."

I hear a scream come across the phone and I'm up out of the chair. It slams against the wall behind me as I grab Tracy by the throat and lift her up with my good arm. Her feet dangle and kick out at me. I can feel the room around me explode with activity, but I care about only one thing, watching her eyes bug out as she fights for breath.

"Linc, we got him." Noah's voice breaks through the fog and I drop her down to the floor.

She chokes for air as we turn and head out of the room. We knew we only had one play, make her think she won so she could call him or tell us where he was. My phone was all set up for the call with Noah's computer hackers waiting to help us. I lost control when she told that asshole he could do whatever he wanted to Rylee. Her scream still rings in my ears as we race toward the elevator and I come to a stop. Traffic is going to be a bitch. We won't be able to get to her on time.

"Come on, I got us a ride," Noah says, and I turn to see him push the roof button.

All of us except Paul and Ollie race across the open roof where a helicopter is landing. I duck down and climb into the back. Zeke jumps in next to me with Noah and Jericho across from us. The commissioner stands to the side of the helipad and waves at us. The helicopter lifts up above the buildings and we are off. Noah reaches into a bag at his feet and pulls out a gun and hands it to me. He knows what I like. I smile at him as I palm the HK P30 9mm. Yeah, he does know me.

"Thanks, man."

"That's what brothers do for each other. Now let's go get your girl."

I turn and look at Jericho and Zeke. Zeke is putting together his rifle. Jericho slides his med kit back and pulls out a shotgun. He straps it to his back, and I notice he has a gun on his hip in a holster too.

"What? Just 'cause I play with fire doesn't mean I don't know how to shoot." He smiles at me. The twenty-five-year old isn't a kid anymore. He's as big as Zeke in height. He doesn't have Zeke's muscle, but he's no small fry. After Kenzie was attacked, he's trained harder and has an edge I've never seen on him before. I reach across and pat his knee.

"Thanks, man," I yell so he can hear me.

"Hey, I thought you were into girls?" He jokes but it doesn't go to his eyes. I look over at Zeke and nod at him. He also just had his girl attacked by a serial killer recently. These guys are really my brothers. When I need them, they have been here for me.

"I just sent a message to Jack; he's got a tracking dog and is working his way toward New Jersey. He's been waiting for me to confirm where. He's ten minutes out from the Palisades Interstate Park area, so he's close."

I nod and push the pain in my shoulder to the back of my mind. I need to get to my girl. The helicopter flies along the Hudson river. We get lower as we pass the park. We know they are somewhere in the northern part of the park. We are passing Hunter's Rock Fall when I spot her. She's struggling with a man on the edge of a cliff. Noah points to something in the distance, and I see Jack approaching with a dog, but I worry we aren't going to be fast enough. Rylee and the man are teetering on the edge. I push for the doorway and watch as Rylee's body separates from the man and he's holding the side of his neck. She falls down and he advances on her with a gun in his other hand as blood rushes down his body.

"Steady." Zeke orders.

Rylee looks over at us. We are close enough now that the down draft of the helicopter is pushing them. She rolls away from the man and further from the edge as I watch him aim the gun at her. He says something to her, and she shakes her head as his head explodes. Zeke sits back after a moment and Noah takes his gun.

"Thank you." I look at him as the pilot tries to find an area where we can land. I keep my eye on Rylee, who Jack has made it to now.

Rylee

CHAPTER
13

It's been a week since the attack. I have nightmares from it. I almost died several times, but I fought to save us both. I've been on bed rest, and Linc pulled his stitches and is on strict activity as well. Christmas was a somber affair, but we were all glad to be together.

I'm leaning back in our massive bed looking outside as the snow slowly falls down. I remember the moment Trajan and I were fighting on the cliff's edge. He hung me over the side and pulled me back. He'd just turned me to head back toward the van when his phone rang. In that moment I struggled with him again when he put the phone on speaker and I heard what Tracy said. I screamed as I used the heels of my boots to attack him. He released me and I ran further away from him, but he caught up with me again and we fought on the edge of that cliff. I stabbed him in the neck with the pen from my purse. I only had one other weapon left, my lancet from my finger prick test kit. I would have used it if I had to. But Trajan's last words to me are what haunt me. He said my father had begged him to kill him and spare my mother. Then Trajan was gone. His face blown away as a shot came from the helicopter. I remember the moment Linc ran up to me. He fell on the ground next to me on his knees and pulled me into his body.

I held him tightly and told him how much I loved him as he told me the same. After that is a blur as we were flown back to the city to a hospital where I was treated for a sprained wrist, bruises, and shock. I had to stay overnight but Linc wouldn't leave my side. Even now he's not far from me. He insists on being with me so much that we had to have the physical therapist come here to our home.

Tomorrow is New Year's Eve and I can't wait for this year to be over. I'm tired of the death and pain. I close my eyes and try to hold the tears in before they flow out and Linc knows I'm worried or scared again.

"Rylee?" a small voice says from the doorway. I open my eyes and turn to look over at Samantha.

"Hey, girly." I smile at her and hope the tears stop.

"Can I come sit with you?" Her head drops and she looks at her feet.

"Of course." She hops up onto the bed and crawls over next to me. "Do you want to watch a movie together?"

"Okay. Can we watch *The Last Unicorn*?"

I reach over and grab the remote that opens the cabinets across the room, and the large flat screen television is revealed. Ever since we got her the movie, she's asked to watch it. I don't mind because it's one of my favorite titles too. She leans back on the pillows and we both escape into the world of make-believe. I'm thinking she's fallen asleep until her little voice starts.

"My dad said I'm going to get to live here with you and him now. Are you going to marry my dad?"

I don't know what he's said to her, but I know in my heart I need to be honest with her.

"Someday I'd like that."

"My mother tried to hurt you and my little brother. Are you mad at me too?" I'm taken aback by her question and pull away from her. She's looking down, not at the movie, and there are tears rolling down her face.

"Samantha, you had nothing to do with the choices your mother made." I carefully pull her body toward me and embrace her. She wraps her arms around me and squeezes me. "I want you to know I'll never treat you any different from your little brother. You're a very special girl and I'd like for you to think of me as someone who cares about you and loves you just like Noah and Kenzie."

"Thank you, Rylee. I love you too." My heart squeezes. In the last week I've given her the space she needs and have just been there when she needed me.

"I love you, Sammy." I choke on the words and hold her tightly.

"Tomorrow can I come to the doctor with you so I can hear the baby's heartbeat too?"

"Yes, you can."

She stays cuddled up to me and we both finish the movie, although we drift off together before it ends.

§.

LINC

I step off the elevator and into the large master suite. I can see the credits rolling on Samantha's movie and turn the corner to see the three most important souls in my world lying together on the bed. My girls have their arms wrapped around each other and my son is nestled between them.

I thought I was going to lose Rylee and my son. I was sure she was going to fall from that cliff. Then I thought the shock would cause her to miscarry, but both held strong and are the miracle I'm blessed to have in my life. My daughter has been the true warrior, though. She wanted to call her mother on Christmas Day, and when I couldn't have her talk to her, I told her the partial truth. But Samantha saw the report on the local news. She cried for only a bit before she told me she had overheard her mother saying she wanted to hurt Rylee, but she didn't know who Rylee was at the time, or that she was carrying her little brother.

I quietly walk across the plush carpet to the far side of the bed. Rylee's side. I slide my hand across her cheek and into her thick dark brown curly hair. She's left it down and has worn no makeup except on Christmas when she said people would see the pictures. Her soft skin is porcelain, and I lean down, unable to stop myself from kissing her full lips. Her eyes flutter open and take me in.

"I couldn't resist."

She smiles and leans up to kiss me again. "I missed you." Her voice is soft, and I watch as she adjusts her arms around Samantha.

I was working out with my physical therapist and then had to meet with the IAD detectives. They wanted to give me the final results. I had already been cleared in the shooting, but they wanted me to know Rocco has been suspended. His job is also in jeopardy unless he comes completely clean with them regarding his involvement in Rylee's kidnapping. I know he wasn't directly involved in it, but he knew Tracy would do anything to get rid of my son.

Tracy feared my parents would split Samantha's shares of the store sale with the baby. What Tracy didn't know was that no matter what, she never would have had any control of the money. It's been put into a trust fund for each of my children, and they can't access it until they are twenty-five.

I also sat down with my parents and discussed the sale. I never thought my father would ever sell, but I understand his need to want to spend time with my mom. As a matter of fact, they are leaving right after the new year for Hawaii and the South Pacific on a second honeymoon they never were able to take. My share of the sale was deposited into an account for me. I tried to give part of it to Rylee for the payment of this house, but she refused and said she'd just put it into an account for the kids. I love how much she does for both of them. If she gets something for the baby, she makes sure Samantha feels included or gets something too.

"Marry me." It's not a question because I'm not letting her tell me no.

She smiles, her eyes dancing. "Not yet."

"I didn't ask, sexy." I tip my head to the side.

"Linc, look at us. I'm on bed rest and you're recovering from being shot."

"It's the perfect time. My parents are here right now."

She shakes her head and tries to turn her face down to look at Samantha. I lift her chin so she's looking up at me.

"Samantha doesn't know me very well and we can't get everything arranged before your parents fly out."

"I've already got it all set up for tomorrow. Told you I was going to marry you. Ollie got you a dress. Just say you will."

"I will." She sighs and I lean down, taking her lips in a deep kiss. I can't wait until I can take her like I want to.

&a.

STANDING in the courtroom with everyone I care about around me, I tell the woman I love that she's mine forever. I've never felt surer of my decision until this moment. Rylee is dressed in a soft cream three-quarter sleeve dress that comes to her knees. The skirt floats over her little belly and she has on a pair of red-and-white T-strap high heels. Her red lipstick is bright against her pale skin. My mother ran to the florist while we went to the doctor for Rylee's checkup. Now Rylee has a bouquet of red and white roses.

Samantha is in a dress Ollie also picked out. It's a retro style white halter top with cherries on it. There's a black belt at the waist and a black crinoline underneath the skirt. She has on little red Mary Jane style shoes, and Rylee even put a victory roll in her hair so they match each other. I look at them and know I'm blessed beyond everything.

When Rylee says I do, and I slide the pear-shaped opal stacking wedding set surrounded by diamonds on her finger, her face lights up and I know I picked right. I only gave her a day to get me a ring, and I'm shocked by the wood and cobalt metal band she picked out. There is a forest etched into the outside of the band and the inside looks like polished pine wood.

After a family dinner with all the Caines at Uncle Romeo's restaurant, we are standing in our bedroom looking out over the night sky.

My hands skate from her shoulders, down her arms, and I turn her around. She leans up and I take her soft lips and explore her mouth. Her body molds against mine as best as she can with my arm strapped to my chest in its brace. I groan and pull away, lifting the Velcro straps to remove it.

"No, Linc, you need to keep it on. Let me take care of you."

She sinks down to her knees in front of me and my breath hitches. I've dreamed of her lips around my cock for months. Her fingers work my belt loose, then the button on my black slacks. After she pulls down the zipper, she slips my pants down my legs along with my boxer briefs. My cock springs out and she presses a kiss against it. When her small hand wraps around the base and slowly pumps up and down, she leans forward to suck off the pearl of precum. I sink my free hand into her hair and start pulling the pins out so I can play with it. Her lips wrap around the tip and she slides down the length, taking a lot of my cock until it bumps the back of her throat. Her eyes stay glued to mine as she pulls back, hollowing out her cheeks. She slips it out of her mouth after a couple times and proceeds to kiss the underside to my balls, where she sucks one then the other into her mouth. I lock my knees to keep me on my feet, but also so I don't blow my load so quickly. It's been months and I've needed her so much.

"Sexy, I want to come inside your tight pussy, not your mouth." I groan trying to maintain control.

She pulls back. "But, Lincoln, we can't."

"Fuck that. Strip and you can ride me." I step back further from her and proceed to remove my brace so I can get my shirt off.

She rises up off the floor and helps me with the buttons because I'm about to rip it from my body. When I'm completely naked, I climb up onto the bed and wait for her. She slips her dress off and I take in the white lacy bra—the cups barely contain her fuller breasts—and her lacy boy shorts that sit right below our son.

"Come here, sexy wife," I growl.

She slips her bra and panties off before taking my hand. I help her up and over me. I want to taste her, but I know she won't sit on my face in my current condition. I pull her face down to me and kiss her, then I slip a finger between her folds. My thumb rubs her clit as I sink two fingers deep into her. She rears back as she moans and rides my fingers, getting herself off. Her breasts bounce and I want to shoot Rocco and the man that shot me for keeping me from my new wife.

Rylee must sense my frustration because she pulls back and lines my cock up with her entrance. She slowly slides down, taking me inch by inch while I lick off my fingers. When she has me deeply seated in her, she moves her body over me, twisting her hips and moving slowly. I use my good arm to push myself up and take a breast into my mouth. Doing everything one-handed is harder but not impossible. I'm going to get my wife off on my cock before I blow like a teenager. She cries out, her head falling back as she pushes me back to the bed.

"Sexy, I need you to come." I groan. "I'm not going to last long."

"Lincoln," she cries out my name as she moves faster, and I snake my hand down to flick her clit. Her hips move faster, and her breasts bounce more as she rides me hard. My eyes about roll back as I feel her squeeze the shit out of my cock and she screams my name. I come, calling her name. She falls to the side as soon as I'm done coming. Her body is pressed up against my right side, my arm around her.

"I love you, Rylee. I know we are fast, but I know we are right."

"I love you too, Lincoln." She drifts off to sleep, and I carefully move to cover her and make sure the house is all locked up from the panel. When I climb back into bed, I'm between the door and her. I'll never take her for granted again. I won't let her be taken or run from me.

Linc

EPILOGUE

LINC

"I need you to push one more time," Dr. Tanner says to Rylee.

Her tired red eyes look at him with sparks of anger in them, then they turn to me.

"Lincoln, I'm too tired. Can we take a break?" she begs me.

"Ry, sexy, I need you to do what Dr. Tanner says. Come on, one more push and our little man will be here."

She's been in labor for hours now, pushing for the last two and she's worn out. I wanted them to do a C-section but Rylee wanted to try. I can't stand to see her in this much pain and struggling. After everything that happened in December, her pregnancy got better. She still had to check her blood sugar, but she never had to go on insulin or other meds. She was able to control her gestational diabetes with diet. But my son is so much bigger than her. Dr. Tanner thinks he's close to nine pounds or more. My poor little wife can't take much more of this.

"Rylee, this last push will do it; the baby is crowning. Here, feel." He grabs her hand and pulls it down between her legs where she can feel our son's head. I look down and see the matted curls. Feeling him must have given her a burst of energy because she pulls up and starts pushing at the next contraction. She cries out as he fully crowns and then pushes again as his shoulders and the rest of his body slides out.

Dr. Tanner places my son on her chest and Rylee

instantly starts crying. I can feel the tears in my eyes and carefully touch his face before I'm directed to cut his umbilical cord. I hold her hand tight and rest my other on his back as she lets Dr. Tanner finish up with her afterbirth and stitching her up.

A nurse walks over and takes him to get weight and tests on him. I watch him but keep Rylee's hand in mine. I lean down and kiss her lips.

"I love you, Ry."

"I love you too, Linc."

"Do we have a name for this boy?" the nurse asks, and we smile at each other.

My father wanted to name all his kids after his favorite presidents. Of course, they only had me, so we decided to continue the tradition.

"Yeah, Theodore Reginald Warren, but we're going to call him Teddy," I say, proud of my son. Named after Teddy Roosevelt and Rylee's dad.

"That's a strong name for this big boy. Nine pounds, six ounces, and twenty-two inches long." She sets him in my arms, and I look down at him. He has a head full of blond curls, his little fists up by his face.

"Okay, you're all cleaned up. Let's get this room back together so we can let that big sister finally come in," Dr. Tanner says. He pats me on the back and chucks my wife under the chin. "You did good, Rylee. I'll check on you guys later."

He walks out and the nurses straighten up the room.

"I want to hold him," Samantha says as soon as the door is opened. She walks over and sits down in the chair next to me. I hand him to her and hover over them both.

"Now that's a big boy." Ollie laughs when he walks in with Paul. They got married last month, much to Rylee's

E.M. SHUE

disappointment. She didn't want to be as big as a house, she said, but they didn't want to wait any longer. They got a case of baby fever and are currently on the list to adopt and are working on finding a house near ours.

My parents travel a lot, but now that Teddy is here, they are going to want to settle near us too. Rylee and I have discussed letting them move into the carriage house after Paul and Ollie move out. Samantha was able to get back into her private school. Her mother is serving time upstate in a prison for her hand in Rylee's kidnapping and attempted murder.

I look over at my wife and see the smile on her face. Every day I show her how much she means to me by telling her and being there for her. I know she still misses her parents, but knowing their murderer paid for his crime with his own life has eased that pain some.

"Rylee, if you and Dad have any more babies, will I have to give up my room?" I look over at Samantha and then back to Rylee.

"Sweetie, it's your home, you don't have to give up your room. And it'll be awhile if your father and I decide to have another baby."

"After this one, I think maybe we should wait and see." I add in. The amount of pain Rylee was in and the fact they almost had to do an emergency C-section scared me too much.

"Knock, knock. Can we come in?" I turn to the door and see Noah and Kenzie with their daughter, Kathleen, at the door.

"Yes, come in," Rylee says in a tired voice. Following right behind them are my parents, along with Zeke and Jamie.

All the women have gotten along so well and have

regular wine nights, or I should say wine for Jamie and water or juice for Kenzie and Rylee.

"I just talked to the bosses. They said take several weeks, we can manage without you," Noah says as he thumps my back.

That was another thing that changed, even though Jeremiah hated losing me as a detective. But I didn't go far. Jeremiah and Securities International created a position for me. I'm a direct liaison between the two entities. Noah moved into the New York East Coast head and I'm the NYPD Liaison. We've created a relationship where when Securities International is protecting dignitaries, we can utilize the NYPD too.

"Thanks, it should only be a couple weeks. Rylee will be kicking me out after that if I know my wife." I pull her hand up to my lips and kiss it as I take in everyone that has become a part of my family as much as I have theirs.

FIVE YEARS LATER

RYLEE

"Mom, I swear if you don't get control of the boys, I will," Sammy yells from the courtyard, and I step out of the main kitchen.

"Boys, leave your sister alone." I huff at them. Teddy is turning five today and our youngest, Reagan, is two. But they aren't happy unless they are making their big sister miserable. Both boys share a room across the hall from Sammy and are constantly invading her seventeen-year-old world.

I look over at her and smile though because I'm going to miss her. She leaves for college this fall. She's graduating a year early and heading to Yale where she got a full-ride scholarship. Linc and Noah are trying to figure out how to put security on her without her knowing. I have to laugh every time because they've failed whenever they've tried it in the past. For her prom they had a guard on her, and she found him within twenty minutes of leaving the house.

"Mom, can I help with anything?" She walks up to me, shaking me from my thoughts.

"No, sweet girl, I've got everything ready already." I pull her in close. Her blond hair is long down her back in waves and she has her dad's crystal blue eyes.

The day she started calling me Mom, I cried for hours. I told Linc I didn't want to replace her mother but just be an addition. Tracy is still in prison and will be for several more years unless something changes. She was convicted of felony murder for hire, on top of many other charges. It wasn't until after Tracy's trial that I found out it was actually Zeke who killed Trajan. Being NYPD and in New Jersey when he killed him, they said it was Noah who shot him so Zeke wouldn't get into trouble. After that day, I spent time with Jamie learning to shoot and fight better than I had already learned. But Linc and the guys want all of us girls to be able to defend ourselves.

When the doorbell rings, I turn to see Linc opening it and watch as the rest of the family all come in. Zeke is hovering over a very pregnant Jamie. They struggled for a long time to get pregnant and when they finally did, it's with twins that are due next month.

Noah and Kenzie arrive with their four kids. Kathleen, Lucas, and twin boys, Asher and Adam. Paul and Ollie walk in next with their three-year-old daughter, Ally. She's the light of their life and keeps both men on their toes. I miss having Ollie living in my backyard, but he now lives a couple blocks away and we see each other every day still.

AFTER EVERYONE HAS LEFT, I step into the shower and let the water from the rainfall shower head splash over my tired body. My eyes are closed and my face raised up trying to cover the tears because my babies are growing up. Hands slide from my hips up to my waist and I'm spun around.

"Sexy, after that phone call this morning, you deserve to be spanked," Linc growls into my ear.

I called Linc and gave him one of his fantasies. I talked to him in my phone sex operator voice, as he calls it. He was in his office at Securities International and I heard him moan out his orgasm as I came. My lips tip up at the memory.

"Oh, Linc, I know you like me to be adventurous." I coo as my hands slide up his slick chest and around his neck. He still turns me on, and I've never felt so cherished or loved before but with him.

"I'll give you adventurous." My back hits the rock wall of our shower and he lifts me up and impales me on his hard cock. I cry out, my head falling back. "Mine, baby. Every fucking inch of you is mine forever."

"Yes," I cry out as he continues to move his cock in and out of me.

"I'm so glad I saw you first before you picked someone else that weekend. My life was just repetition of the day before. You broke me out and into the light and beauty that is you."

"You were the one that saved me. I wasn't even living before you." I lean forward and take his lips. He pulls out and turns me around. He never fails to make me orgasm so hard I feel my heart stop, and this time is no different.

"Hands on the bench." He orders, and I bend over presenting my ass to him as my hands grip the edge of the bench.

"Fuck, I love this ass." His hands slide across it before he slides into me again. Moving harder and faster than before.

After I had Reagan, he got himself fixed because he didn't want to get me pregnant again. Reagan was just as big as Teddy, but I had to have him via C-section because they didn't want me to go through as much as I did before.

His cock hits that spot inside me and I immediately see stars. I scream my orgasm as I feel his body tighten behind me and he growls my name.

"I love you, Ry," he says as he pulls me up, my back to his chest.

"I love you, Lincoln."

ABOUT THE AUTHOR

Writer, wife and mother of three girls. This multi-published author likes her whiskey Irish, her chocolate dark and her hockey hard hitting. She's an avid reader and you can find her Kindle packed full of all sub-genres of romance. When she isn't writing action-adventure, suspense, and strong woman she's spending time with her husband and three daughters.

She's currently writing the hot and steamy romantic suspense series Securities International and the novella series The Caine & Graco Saga. Her first two books in the Securities International series have both won the Colorado RWA Beverley contest, Sniper's Kiss in 2018 for Suspense, and Angel's Kiss in 2019 for Contemporary.

E.M.'s favorite saying is don't piss her off she'll write you into a book and kill you off in a new and gory way.

Join Cocktails & Friends to be kept up to date. https://bit.ly/EMDrinkswithfriends

ACKNOWLEDGMENTS

Here we are again, 2020 has been a busy year for me with releases and I'm super excited I was able to get you this story. It started out as a story that was going to be in an anthology but with all the postponements this year for signings, I was able to move it into a full story for you, my readers.

I want to thank my Lord for giving this talent and for the ability to stay home and write full-time.

First on this long list is the most important person, my husband, without him I wouldn't be doing this crazy thing called writing. My family is the reason I wake up every morning and expose my inner thoughts to you all.

My daughters are second, all of you are the reason my heroines are so strong. I'm proud of each of you and thank God every day for you. Thank you for all your help and support. Paige, you're becoming an awesome PA and I appreciate all your hard work. Kelsey, thank you for your help and support. Dani, thank you for listening to all these crazy storylines. Thank you!!

As always thank you to my support system Krystal Fahl, Dawn Shue, and Tania Gray, you ladies put up with my crazy and talk me down when I need it. Thank you to all of you for everything you put up with. Krystal thank you for also being one of my writing bitches, between you and AJ you motivate me to get the words down.

To all my extended family, brothers, sisters, mom, mother-in-law, cousins, fosters, and those extras that I call family thank you always for your support.

Nadine you're not only my editor but you've become one of my closest friends. Thank you for all your help and support.

Leah, thank you for another beautiful cover.

Thank you to all the authors in all the support chats we have. I'm glad to be a part of each and everyone of these.

My Street and ARC teams, thank you for all your support through postings and reading my words before others do.

Finally, to you the reader, each book I write I think of you. It's because of you that I continue, as long as someone is willing to read, I'll keep writing the stories. Thank you for your support! Hopefully we'll see each other at a signing when the world gets off lockdown.

Made in the USA
Columbia, SC
30 September 2020